Bracebridge Hemyng

The season at Brighton

A romance of fashionable life

Bracebridge Hemyng

The season at Brighton
A romance of fashionable life

ISBN/EAN: 9783337197728

Printed in Europe, USA, Canada, Australia, Japan

Cover: Foto ©Andreas Hilbeck / pixelio.de

More available books at **www.hansebooks.com**

THE

SEASON AT BRIGHTON

PRICE ONE SHILLING

THE

SEASON AT BRIGHTON.

A Romance of Fashionable Life.

BY

BRACEBRIDGE HEMYNG,

AUTHOR OF "THE MAN OF THE PERIOD," "ETON SCHOOL-DAYS," "CALLED TO THE BAR,"
ETC. ETC.

LONDON:

WARD, LOCK, AND TYLER,

WARWICK HOUSE, PATERNOSTER ROW.

AND ALL BOOKSELLERS AND RAILWAY STATIONS.

CONTENTS.

THE

SEASON AT BRIGHTON.

CHAPTER I.

THE MYSTERIOUS DOCTOR.

SIR HAROLD EVANDER, a rich and handsome gentleman, succeeded to the title and estates of his father at
the early age of six-and-twenty.

Unhappily he was impregnated with the love of those
vices which have ruined so many belonging to our aris-
tocracy, and the new baronet speedily began to shine on
the turf, and in certain circles to which nothing but the
most reckless extravagances will gain admittance.

His friends were justly alarmed at the headlong
manner in which they saw that he was rushing to destruction.   It is true that the estates were entailed, and
he could not alienate them; but he was rapidly spend-
ing the large sum of ready-money which his deceased
father had during many years accumulated, and threatened to encumber himself with debts which could only
in the end involve him in disastrous ruin.

B

This being the case, it was decided by those members of the family who had his welfare really at heart, that the only thing which could save him from utter destruction was his marriage with some good and virtuous lady, who would exercise a judicious control over his actions, and gradually wean him from his evil courses and vicious company.

There was but one woman in the society in which he moved who had attracted him in the least, and this was Agneta, the daughter of a poor gentleman named Bannister, the younger son of a good family, whose elder brother had, according to our law of primogeniture, inherited everything at the death of their father, to the exclusion of the remaining children.

Agneta was very lovely and very proud. She detested poverty, because she had suffered terribly all her life from its crushing influence, and she was determined to marry well. It could not be said that she possessed an affectionate disposition; for she had been brought up in a hard school, in which the gentler attributes of a woman's nature were deadened, if not obliterated.

Sir Harold Evander was struck with her beauty, and thought that she would be a desirable addition to his household. His conduct on the occasion of his making a proposal to her for her hand was very much like that of a man bidding for a handsome horse to place in his stable, or of bargaining for a magnificent work of art, or a splendid piece of furniture, which he thinks would render his home luxurious to his admiring friends. He offered her the solid advantages which undoubtedly accrue to the wife of a man of independent fortune; and she, being completely mercenary, gladly accepted his offer, though he had reason to doubt the sincerity of her passion.

In fact, he speedily found that, though he had married the woman, he did not possess her heart. This was not the fault of Agneta. Rather should her education be blamed, for, in sober truth, she had no heart to give him.

She presided with majestic dignity at his parties; she was agreeable to his friends—rather too much so occasionally, he could not help thinking; and she aided him in his extravagance to such a degree, that, to use a homely expression, the candle was very soon burning at both ends and in the middle.

Home possessed no greater attraction for Sir Harold Evander after his marriage than it did before. The coldness of his wife's manner repelled him; he came to regard her as a beautiful statue, and was satisfied so long as he knew she was in her place.

His occasional absences were prolonged. Instead of staying at Newmarket, and other places where sporting men congregate, a week, he would stay away double that time; and, feeling lonely, the Lady Agneta Evander betook herself to Brighton, Cheltenham, and other fashionable places, where she could enjoy the society of people in her own position, and display the magnificence of her toilet and the almost inexhaustible resources of her crowded wardrobe, which were lost in the dismal solitude of a country house. Of course, a lady young, handsome, rich, could not long remain without admirers. Wheresoever she went, lovers sighed at her feet, but she gave them no encouragement; a stony stare rewarded their complimentary speeches, and gathering up the skirts of her dress, as if she would be defiled by contact with her flatterers, she swept majestically away, leaving the wretched men without hope.

The most persistent follower who pestered her with his presence was a remarkable man, about thirty years of age, who was known as Dr. Rox. That he was possessed of money no one could doubt, as he lived well, paid promptly for everything that he had, never practised in his profession, and yet was easy and unconcerned in his manner.

That he was clever, even the first physicians in Brighton admitted, because he once cured a Russian princess after she had been given over by her attendants. His conversation was that of a well-educated, deeply-read, and polished gentleman, who had travelled in most quarters of the globe. In stature Dr. Rox was small, compactly made, with regular and intelligent features; but his complexion was of an olive tint, and though he declared himself an Englishman, he might just as well have been taken for a native of the Brazils. He spoke several languages fluently, and had the most wonderful eyes that ever scintillated and glittered out of the head of a snake.

His eyes had the singular power of fascinating all upon whom he chose to fix them attentively; there was a charm in them. They seemed to dart a subtle species of magnetism into another, which compelled that one to own the attraction, and submit humbly to the superior power which held him in thrall.

Those who had travelled in Italy, where superstition is rife and sways most minds, declared that he had the evil eye; but the majority of the ladies whom he favoured with his glances would not admit that there was anything malignant in them.

If Lady Agneta Evander sojourned at Bath, there also would be the mysterious doctor; did she go to Brighton, he would, by a species of divination, discover her whereabouts, and instantly visit the scene. Nowhere could she be free from him, unless she buried herself in the recesses of her country house, which nothing could induce her to do.

Sir Harold Evander had a horse entered for one of the great races, and he staked immense sums upon its success. As usual, he went away from home to attend to his affairs and enjoy his favourite pastime. Lady Agneta departed the same evening for Brighton.

Three days elapsed, and, to her surprise, she saw nothing of the doctor, who usually followed as her shadow. While out riding, attended only by her groom, she could not help thinking of this pertinacious admirer, who, in spite of a succession of rebuffs, which would have discouraged any ordinary being, still persisted in haunting her path.

Although early in the day, the sun had shone out with great power, but heavy banks of clouds drifted up from the sea and obscured its disc. The wind moaned fitfully, and suddenly ceased altogether; the ocean became calm as a vast inland lake, and it was evident that one of those convulsions of nature so frequent in summer was at hand. On one side of the road stretched the expanse of interminable downs, upon which some sheep were browsing; on the other, separated from the highway by a narrow strip of grass, was the edge of the precipitous cliffs, which sloped down to the sea.

The horse ridden by Lady Agneta was a tall, handsome, high-spirited animal, which had not been long in her possession. Her groom, seeing the threatening aspect of the weather, thought it advisable to urge his mistress to return, as he dreaded the effect of the coming storm upon so fiery a creature as the one she was on.

Cantering up, he touched his hat and ventured to say,

"I beg your pardon, my lady, but the horse may shy if the thunder comes on suddenly."

"I am not afraid," answered Lady Evander carelessly; "any one would think, from your nervous manner, that I was only just learning to ride."

"Better turn back, my lady, if I may presume so far as to say so," continued the groom; "the cliffs are close to us, and very dangerous to a runaway horse."

A shade of displeasure crossed Lady Agneta Evander's face; she waved the man back impatiently, and struck the horse sharply on the flank with her whip.

At the same moment a terrific clap of thunder burst over their heads, immediately preceded by a peculiarly vivid flash of lightning.

The roar of the thunder was like the explosion of a park of artillery, and shook the very ground. The darkness increased, and heavy drops of rain splashed on the parched ground.

Roused by the lash of the whip, and alarmed by the roar of the thunder, the horse erected his ears and trembled convulsively.

Another flash, followed by a second report, louder and nearer than the first, completed his panic, and, throwing his ears back, he took the bit in his mouth, and dashed forward at a terrible pace.

In vain her ladyship tried to stop his flight; fruitless were the efforts of the groom to overtake her. On

like the wind flew the frightened steed, and, with
blanched cheeks and parted lips, Agneta owned to herself the danger of her position, which was produced by
her own temerity and reckless disregard of a probable
peril.

Jumping some rails by the roadside, the maddened
steed rushed wildly along the edge of the cliff, threatening every moment to make a false step, or swerve a
little to the right, which would have had the effect of
precipitating his rider and himself into the abyss, where
they would infallibly have been dashed to pieces on the
rocks below.

While her nerves were wrought to their highest
capacity of tension, and she feared momentarily to fall
a victim to an awful death, the apparition of a horseman
in front of her cheered her drooping spirits, and inspired
her with a hope to which for the last ten dreadful
minutes she had been a stranger. The horseman had
reined-in his steed, which he bestrode firmly. Lady
Agneta could not help passing him, and he was evidently waiting for her to do so.

Furiously raged the storm.

The lightning flashes were more frequent, vivid,
and blinding. The clouds dashed against each other in
frantic anger, producing an awe-inspiring music of the
elements calculated to deafen mankind.

Utterly regardless of this, the man on horseback
kept his eyes fixed upon the runaway animal, which
approached him with the rush of a whirlwind.

Leaping up lightly in his saddle, this man, who was
indeed to be her ladyship's preserver, extended his arm,
and as she passed him, dexterously snatched her from
her perilous position.

At the same instant her horse, additionally alarmed at this interruption to his impetuous career, made the fatal swerve which had impended twenty times before, and, slipping over the edge of the cliff, rolled down the steep incline till he fell with a dull heavy thud upon some jagged rocks beneath, and lay there mangled—dead.

Lady Evander fainted.

She could bear no more; and seeing that her senses had left her, her saviour gently placed her body on the greensward, and awaited her recovery from this temporary evanishment.

The groom, who never expected to see his mistress alive again, now galloped up, his face radiant with smiles, and touched his hat to the gentleman, who told him to hold his horse.

Having expended its violence in that particular spot, the storm rolled sullenly on in the direction of Brighton; a few large drops continued to fall upon the ground and watered the upturned face of Lady Agneta, contributing by their cooling influence to her recovery, which soon took place.

Looking around her, she found herself supported in the encircling arms of Dr. Rox,—for it was he who had so courageously, and with such consummate skill, saved her life.

In a moment, the scene which had just taken place flashed across her memory. Gently disengaging herself from his support, she rose to her feet, and thanked him without any appearance of cordiality for the service he had rendered her. She had already renewed her habitual coldness, and the calm and icy smile, which even seemed to mock those around her, sat on her lips, and she regarded her preserver with a species of impertinent curiosity.

"You were very nearly quitting this gay and festive scene for ever, Lady Evander," exclaimed Dr. Rox gravely; "but I am happy that my poor exertions have saved the heart of your husband from desolation."

A sarcastic smile, which well matched her own, accompanied these words, and brought an angry flush to her ladyship's cheeks. She looked about her, as if wondering how she should get back to Brighton.

Divining her thoughts, the doctor added :

"Permit me to suggest that your groom should ride back to the town and despatch a fly for your convenience. I will in the mean time, with your permission, offer my arm, walk along the road with, and assist you to meet the carriage."

Her ladyship favoured him with a frigid bow. The doctor gave the groom his instructions, and the man rode off at a brisk pace, leading the other horse by the bridle. Placing her hand within his arm, Lady Evander walked to the road, and they took the direction of the town, towards which the groom could be faintly distinguished in the distance, riding at as good a pace as his jaded horse could carry him.

The doctor was fond of studying character, and he fancied that her ladyship would well repay his investigation. She on her part was piqued to know who and what man this was.

They were both occupied with their own thoughts, and as they proceeded the silence grew oppressive.

Lady Evander was the first to break it.

"May I ask you, doctor," she exclaimed, "why you hang like a shadow upon my footsteps?"

"I have no objection to answer the question, though some would consider it an impertinent, not to say an embarrassing one," he rejoined.

"It is I who should complain of an intolerable annoyance," said the lady.

"What," exclaimed the doctor, "may not the mote bask in the sunbeam? You may forbid me to speak to you, but it is impossible that you can banish me from the sunshine of your presence, unless you shut yourself up in a prison. Had you considered yourself really annoyed by seeing me constantly following you, what course would you have adopted? you would have told your husband, who holds you a little dearer than he does his dogs and horses. Between you and Sir Harold Evander there is no sympathy; but between you and I there exists a mutual though tacit understanding."

"I do not understand you," said Lady Evander, whose face betrayed the astonishment she felt.

"Let me hasten to explain. It has been truly said by an astute philosopher, that every living being in this world has an exact counterpart of himself—not bodily, but in tastes, disposition, mind. It may be that these two never meet; when they do, they cannot fail to exert an occult and mysterious influence over each other, their destinies become united. Perhaps, Lady Evander, you will say you never yet met your double?"

"Never," she replied emphatically; "nor do I think it likely, as I am not a believer in your strange theory."

"Some day you will confess its truth. Even now you deceive yourself, for I assert that you have met this representation of yourself, in the shape of a man who has come from the antipodes. This double, Lady Evander, is myself."

As Dr. Rox uttered these words, he stopped, and disengaging her hand from his arm, drew himself up and gazed intently at her, she trembling like a bird before his ardent look.

Recovering herself, she exclaimed :

" I have hitherto regarded you, sir, as a gentleman, possessed of talent in your profession. I shall henceforth consider you extremely impertinent."

Not in the least disconcerted at this energetic address, the doctor pointed to a carriage coming along the road.

" There is your conveyance, Lady Evander. I shall now have to leave you, but rest assured we shall meet again. Our destinies are inseparably united in the future. Laugh at me—insult me, if you will! I speak with prophetic voice. The time is not far distant when you will send for me. I shall come, and that you may make sure of finding me in your hour of need, this for a time will be my address: The St. James's Hotel, Piccadilly, London."

Lifting his hat politely, Dr. Rox took his leave of Lady Evander, whom he left confounded by his assurance, and jumping lightly over a small hedge, walked over the downs in the direction of Lewes.

It did not seem possible to Agneta that she should ever be reduced to such a strait as that sketched by the doctor. Her distress must be great indeed to induce her to send for one who was morally and physically repulsive to her.

Yet he was right.

Events had been occurring during the last four-and-twenty hours which were destined to alter the course of her existence in a material degree.

In the afternoon there was a concert at the Pavilion. Here those who were in the fashionable world congregated. Lady Evander was present, proud and isolated as was her wont.

Two gentlemen stopped behind her chair as they were promenading to and fro, and began to converse. One exclaimed:

"I am sorry for Evander. His horse was beaten by a short head, and they say that he is utterly ruined. He staked all he possessed on the event."

"He has the entailed estates still," observed the other.

"That is true, but the revenue will only enable him to live abroad. His income from that source cannot be more than three or four thousand a-year, and he is so involved that he can never hold up his head again in England. If he has not already decamped, he will soon be arrested for debt."

"A pleasant prospect for his wife, truly! By the way, I hear she is staying down here now."

Then they passed on.

Lady Evander's heart sank within her. Desperate, indeed, must her unfortunate husband's position be, if his calamities were already in every one's mouth. But worse was to come.

Before the night fell she was thinking of the doctor and his weird prediction.

Was he, indeed, her double? and were their destinies united, as he had ventured to assert?

That evening she received a telegram from her country house, despatched by the steward. The contents were terribly concise, but well calculated to alarm her already agitated mind.

"Please, my lady, come home at once. Sir Harold is dangerously ill."

Her husband ill! Those words threatened her with a tangible calamity; for should Sir Harold Evander die, she would once more be penniless and obscure. All his available property was dissipated. She had no children, and the entailed estates would pass into the hands of a relation, whom she had offended by her haughty behaviour, and who was in consequence her deadly enemy.

Scant pity and consideration could she expect from him.

It was impossible for her to sleep that night; so she ordered horses to be put to the carriage, and posted towards her country home, so that she might save a few hours by not waiting for the morning.

The time had been when she despised that ancient mansion, hidden amongst the splendid timber of the spacious park; but now that there was a chance, as she thought, of its passing out of her hands for ever, it became inexpressibly precious to her, and she felt that she could commit a crime, if need be, to retain possession of it.

On entering the house her appearance was wild and haggard, and the family physician, who met her in the porch, attributed her distress to the anxiety which she would naturally feel at finding her husband ill.

"Pray be calm, my lady," exclaimed Dr. Wethered; "we must not anticipate the worst. There may be—"

"Is my husband dying?" she queried, in a voice that trembled with ill-suppressed emotion.

"We have done our best. Medical science can do no more. My brother physicians and I have been in

consultation; but it is my painful duty, Lady Evander,
to prepare you for a catastrophe, should the fever which
has supervened take an unfavourable turn."

" In other words, you have given Sir Harold up. I
thank you for your candour, sir."

Lady Evander passed him by with an inclination of
the head, and entering the drawing-room rang the bell
violently.

The steward, who had been awaiting this summons,
immediately answered it.

During the time that elapsed between the ringing
of the bell and the appearance of the steward she had
hastily written on a sheet of note-paper:

" The Moat, Sussex.—To Dr. Rox, St. James's Hotel, Piccadilly, London: Come to me here at once, I
implore you. Sir Harold is dying. You alone can
save him."

"Take this directly, Hammond, to the station, and
transmit it to town by telegraph," handing the paper to
the steward. " Go yourself, if you please, and ride one
of the fastest horses in the stable; your master's life
perhaps may depend upon your speed."

The steward was one of those invaluable men who
prefer acting to talking, and without a word he bowed
and left the room. In five minutes he was careering
with the wind on the road to the railway station, where
there was a telegraph office.

The message was despatched.

Lady Evander sat like a statue in the drawing-room.
She would see no one, ask no questions, nor did she
evince any signs of vitality, so quiet and insensible was
she.

Three hours elapsed.

Hammond had returned more leisurely than he went, but he had not been home long before a mounted messenger arrived with a telegraphic message. It was an answer to her own, and contained the one word "Hope." When Lady Evander read it her countenance brightened. She thanked the steward for the quick despatch he had made, and began to question him respecting the cause of her husband's illness.

CHAPTER II.

THE DEEP PLOT.

"HOPE."

That one word, dispatched by the mysterious doctor to her own urgent solicitation for his presence, and which had reached him with electric speed, raised Lady Evander from the depth of despair into which she had been plunged on hearing of her husband's danger.

Dr. Wethered remained on the premises; but he was so much offended by the cold and disdainful manner in which her ladyship had treated him, that he did not again seek her presence.

Indeed his patient, who was rapidly sinking, required all his care and attention.

The story which Hammond the steward had to tell the Lady Agneta was as brief as it was sad and melancholy.

Sir Harold returned from the races half mad with excitement, consequent on the heavy losses he had sustained through the defeat of his favourite horse, which had been beaten at the post by a mere nothing.

He called for brandy, and drank deeply. Hammond saw him in the morning, and he did not appear to have slept an hour during the whole of that long and wretched night.

Eating nothing, and continuing to drink, heightened the desperation of Sir Harold Evander, who, towards noon, shut himself up in the library. Hammond applied for admittance, which was refused him.

Half-an-hour afterwards a loud report, which startled the whole household, was heard.

Hammond, at the head of the domestics, rushed upstairs, and with difficulty broke open the locked door.

A dreadful sight presented itself to their affrighted gaze, for Sir Harold Evander was stretched on the crimsoned floor, terribly wounded by a bullet which had perforated his chest and penetrated to his lungs.

That he had attempted to commit suicide there was not the slightest shadow of a doubt.

Doctors were sent for in hot haste, and Sir Harold Evander, deathly pale, still alive, his handsome countenance convulsed with pain, was taken upstairs and placed on a bed.

His condition grew hourly worse. The ball was extracted, but the physicians gave faint hopes of his recovery.

It was in this melancholy state that Lady Agneta found him, when, preceded by Hammond, she entered the apartment which soon threatened to be the chamber of death. She sat down by the bedside and endeavoured to make her husband recognise her; but he returned her seemingly affectionate gaze with a glassy stare.

He' was all in all to the cold, heartless, mercenary woman now, because his untimely decease would reduce her to penury, and she could not brook the idea of returning a poor dependent to her family.

In the height of her prosperity she had treated them with a disdain which their former kindness did not merit; when they called upon her, she received them as if they had been beggars, and refused to give them any assistance out of her store of plenty.

What a triumph for them would her degradation be! and how bitter would taste the bread she would, by the decrees of fate, be obliged to receive at their hands!

Dr. Rox was her only hope, and with a fierce impatience she counted the minutes until his arrival.

While she was waiting in this feverish excitement, Dr. Wethered entered the room. He bowed stiffly to Lady Evander, and examined his patient, who seemed sunk in a state of lethargy.

Lady Agneta interrogated him with her eyes, and he exclaimed,

" Sir Harold Evander has but a few hours to live. It is best that your ladyship should know this. I can do no more; human skill is of no avail."

" Thank you for your kind attention to my poor husband," replied Lady Evander, in a stony voice. " I have, however, sent for my own physician from London, out of no intentional disrespect to you, and expect him here shortly."

" In that case I shall withdraw," answered Dr. Wethered, whose countenance betrayed the displeasure

C

he felt. "Up to the last moment I will attend upon Sir Harold; but when another medical man, a stranger to myself, usurps your confidence and enters this apartment, I consider that I shall be wanting in respect to myself if I remain."

"By your own confession, Dr. Wethered, you can be of no further use," answered Lady Evander; "therefore you have my perfect permission to act as you please."

Dr. Wethered remained in the room until evening, when the wheels of a carriage were heard grating on the gravel in front of the house, and Dr. Rox arrived.

The steward announced him, and Dr. Wethered took his departure, as he had threatened.

Lady Evander uttered a cry of joy as the mysterious stranger entered the room.

"Doctor," she exclaimed, "if you can save my husband's life, I shall be eternally indebted to you!"

An ironical smile rose to his well-cut lips as he approached the bed, making no reply to the words which her ladyship had addressed to him. She followed him with her eyes, and watched him turn down the coverlid and lay his hand upon the heart of the dying man. Turning round, he exclaimed,

"You must admit, Lady Evander, that I was right when I said the other day at Brighton that you would soon have need of me."

"Save my husband!" she answered in a plaintive voice.

With the utmost deliberation he examined the wound, then, re-covering the body of Sir Harold Evander, he said with a grave shake of the head, "He is doomed."

"O, do not say that!" cried the Lady Agneta, in a voice which was laden with terror, for the sentence of death fell upon her like a knell, and overwhelmed her with its force.

"Why trifle with your feelings?" said Dr. Rox, with phlegm. "Sir Harold Evander is already hesitating on the brink of the next world. Why should I raise delusive hopes in your breast?"

"If I only had a son!" murmured the wretched woman.

"Ah!" exclaimed the doctor, "now you are becoming practical. If you had a son, you would be its guardian, and the settled property would not pass away from you to vest in strangers. Let us talk as if we were alone."

Lady Evander cast an affrighted glance in the direction of the bed.

"Do not be alarmed," said Dr. Rox. "Your husband is not yet dead, but he is unconscious. His time is short on earth, and if you are wise, you will look the situation in the face. You do not love Sir Harold. It is not possible for you to love anybody. It is not the man, but the loss of position and fortune that you regret."

Lady Evander covered her face with her hands, and wept bitterly.

This man's raillery cut her to the heart, because it humbled her pride, and humiliation of that kind was a sort of moral death to her.

"I have a proposition to make to your ladyship," resumed the doctor.

She looked up, regarding him attentively.

"If within a certain time after the death of Sir

Harold Evander it is notified to the world that you have borne a son, the entailed estates will be his, and you, being his guardian, will have the enjoyment of the property until he comes of age."

" Well!" she ejaculated in a stony voice.

" You shall retire into the country, and live a secluded life for some months. When the proper time has arrived, I will provide a child, which shall pass as that of Sir Harold and yourself. By carefully following my instructions, the fraud which we shall jointly perpetrate on the next heir cannot be discovered. The baby which I undertake to provide shall be by every one considered your own, and by this means you will be able to claim the property for your offspring."

Her ladyship looked at him as if she could scarcely believe the evidence of her senses.

" There is, however, one condition which I must stipulate for," continued the doctor.

" Which is—"

" This. You are a woman without heart or feeling. Bring this child up to resemble yourself and me. That little thing which beats under the left breast, and which men call a heart, is a superfluous luxury to men of the world. I will promise you that the parentage of this child, which I am going to bring you, shall fit him for the part which I wish him to play, if you will second my efforts."

" But," exclaimed Lady Agneta with a shudder she could not repress, " you will, like Frankenstein, create a demon which you will want to destroy."

" Perhaps," he answered, with a diabolical smile. " Those who create have a right to destroy."

At that moment there was something so fiend-like

in the face of the mysterious doctor, that Lady Evander was compelled to turn away her eyes.

"Well," she said at last, "I consent. O yes; I would consent to anything rather than submit to that awful poverty which I dread so much, and dread all the more through having already experienced its bitterness. After all, those who have no heart are the happiest in this world."

"Always provided they have money," supplemented Dr. Rox; adding, with his sarcastic smile: "It shall not be my fault if you do not have a happy man in your son."

The dying man moved uneasily in his bed, as if the words had made the waning spark of life flicker momentarily with a stronger flame.

"I place myself unreservedly in your hands," said Lady Evander.

"That is a necessity from which, in the present emergency, you could not escape. In a short time you shall see me again. Business of importance calls me for a few weeks to the East. When I return from Constantinople I will wait upon your ladyship."

With more than his usual politeness, Dr. Rox took his leave; and Lady Evander, bestowing one hurried look upon her dying husband, quitted the apartment, which for her was filled with gloomy anticipations and vain regrets.

Hammond met his mistress on the stairs, and gave her to understand that he had prepared dinner, begging her, for the sake of her health, to eat something.

"Has Dr. Wethered left the house?" she inquired.

"Not yet, my lady," answered Hammond; "his horse is being harnessed now."

"Give him my compliments, and say I shall be glad of his company."

A slight repast had been got ready by the attentive Hammond, which was placed on the table just as Dr. Wethered came in.

"Pray, doctor," said Lady Evander, in her most winning accents, "forgive me if I was in any way rude to you just now. Consider my position, and the horrible anxiety with which I am tormented. Dr. Rox has gone back to town. He quite approved of your treatment, but regards my unhappy husband's case as hopeless."

Considerably mollified, Dr. Wethered consented to stay to dinner, and carved a fowl for her ladyship, who ate sparingly. At times her tears would burst out as if she had no control over her crying, and the good doctor felt sincerely sorry for her.

"It is such a blow to me," she sobbed; "especially as—as—I may tell you, doctor, that Sir Harold's fondest hopes would soon have been realised."

At this intelligence the doctor positively started in his chair.

"That is good news," he said, looking at Lady Evander, whose eyes were cast down in modest confusion. "I am glad to hear the Moat will not pass into the hands of strangers, which will not happen should Sir Harold have a son and heir."

"We are all in the hands of fate," answered her ladyship abstractedly; adding, "Will you communicate what I have just told you, my good friend, to Mr. Bellamy, our solicitor—that is to say, should our worst fears be confirmed? It is only fair that Mr. George Evander, who is the heir-at-law, I believe, should not be buoyed-up with false hopes."

" Quite so. I entirely agree with your ladyship, and approve of your consideration and forethought. Of course, the event may disappoint our expectations. It may be a girl, instead of a boy, and a female cannot take an entailed estate. Still, we will hope for the best, and I should be indeed sorry if any word of mine damped your anticipations. I will see Mr. Bellamy, who, in due course, will write to Mr. George."

Lady Agneta thanked the doctor for his kindness, and expressed a wish to be alone, begging that she might be called at once should there be any change, either for better or worse, in the condition of the patient.

She retired to her boudoir, in which a lamp, pendent from the ceiling, shed a dim religious light throughout the exquisitely-furnished apartment. With a cruel hard smile, she said to herself:

" If Dr. Rox could have heard me, he would give me credit for possessing some of his talent for intrigue. Every one will soon know that there is a probability of my presenting a son to the world."

For hours she sat alone, revolving many things in her mind, and indulging ambitious thoughts.

Midnight came.

There was a subdued knocking at the door, and in a faint voice she murmured,

" Come in."

Dr. Wethered was the intruder upon her ladyship's privacy. His face was calm, but grave. She well knew the mission upon which he had come; nevertheless she interrogated him with her eyes.

" All is over," said the doctor. " He has passed from amongst us peacefully."

" It is Heaven's will," replied Lady Evander, with a hypocritical pretence of resignation.

Dr. Wethered did all in his power to console the young and lovely widow, and was more successful than he had expected to be.

An hour afterwards she retired to her bedchamber, and the night went on in that oppressive stillness which always reigns when there is death in a house.

Ere her eyes closed in sleep, she ejaculated:

"Now all my hopes are fixed upon the skill of Dr. Rox, and the credulity of those who surround me."

CHAPTER III.

HOW THE FRAUD WAS ACCOMPLISHED.

DR. WETHERED was not slow in communicating the delicate intelligence Lady Evander had made him the recipient of to Mr. Bellamy, the family solicitor, who was much surprised at what he heard. The doctor had timed his visit early in the morning, and the attorney was at breakfast; he had heard the melancholy news of Sir Harold Evander's death, and was prepared for it. After breakfast he intended to start for the Moat, and affix seals upon all cupboards, boxes, &c. which might contain valuable documents or property.

Pouring out a cup of coffee—for he was a single man, and had no gentle helpmate to preside at his table —Mr. Bellamy, addressing the physician, said,

"Of course I can have no possible reason for doubting the truth of what you have just told me. The birth of a child will alter the complexion of affairs very materially; but from my knowledge of Mr. George Evander's character, I do not think he will acquiesce quietly in the new state of affairs. He wrote me yesterday that he was coming to the Moat to-day, and hoped to see his unfortunate relation before he expired."

"Supposing the child to be a son," replied Dr. Wethered, "Mr. George will have no title to the estates or the baronetcy—at least, I should think not. I appeal to you, being lamentably ignorant on legal questions."

"It is useless to discuss the matter until the event takes place," answered Mr. Bellamy. "My advice to Lady Evander will be to retire to some out-of-the-way place, and lead a secluded life, until she can emerge with her son and claim everything. If I were to have the management of her affairs—and I suppose she will intrust them to me—I should recommend her to let Mr. George Evander enter on possession of the Moat, duly notifying him of the probable eventuality. Ejection, if he is obstinate, will be easy enough when we have the power and are in a position to dictate terms."

"That is true enough," said the doctor, who was quite satisfied with this mode of reasoning.

Lady Agneta Evander was perfectly willing to do as her solicitor advised her. After the funeral she removed to a remote seaside village in Norfolk, being recommended to do so in a letter she received from Dr. Rox. Mr. George Evander was allowed to take up his abode at the Moat and enjoy the title for a time, though he felt very uneasy at the prospect before him, praying devoutly that her ladyship's offspring might prove a daughter. The merest chance in the world would decide whether he was to remain a man of property and a baronet, or return to the obscurity from which he had emerged to dazzle his neighbours and friends with a transient splendour.

The spot which Lady Agneta had selected for her retirement was kept a profound secret from every one except Mr. Bellamy, who, being requested not to do so, would not betray the confidence reposed in him on any account. Had Sir George Evander known where she was, he would have surrounded her with spies, and her every movement would have been carefully watched.

In the mean time Dr. Rox was not idle. The month of November had, in its early part, failed to bring with it the fogs we associate with its name. The days were fine, and the nights cold with frost. The doctor took a fancy for duck-shooting, and went to the east coast, where there were broad sheets of water in the fen country covered with wild-fowl—sheldrakes, ruffs, and reeves, with troops of shore-larks. The cry of the curlew and the peewit was heard, and the dove-like gulls flew over from the rolling waves of the German Ocean.

A stout sea wall in many cases protected the low lands from the lagoon-like "broads" or lakes, and a peculiarity of the country consisted in a number of small low marsh-mills, dotting the land here and there, and pumping the water out of the ditches into the lakes, which acted the part of reservoirs.

In one of these mills lived a man and his wife. They had not been married more than a year, and were daily expecting a child to bless their union, which hitherto had been a very happy one.

During his peregrinations over the marshy country, Dr. Rox frequently paid a visit to this man Fryer and his wife Mary. He made them little presents, brought

them a bottle of spirits occasionally, and sometimes partook of their frugal fare, the offering of which was the
only return they were able to make for his continued
and, as far as their experience went, unusual kindness.
There was a terrible storm one night, which did a deal
of damage in the neighbourhood. The country could
not be called well wooded, but many a pollard willow
was laid low, and the water in the large "broad" was
lashed into foam, and beat wildly against the wall which
kept it from inundating the surrounding country.

A large flour-mill, which ground corn for everybody
for miles round, was injured about one of its sails, and
the miller sent for Fryer to come and repair the damage,
mending the sails of windmills being one of the things
which Fryer could do well. The man was just starting
on his expedition, when Dr. Rox hove in sight, carrying
his long-barrelled duck-gun on his shoulder. The morning was fine and calm, scarcely a breath of wind ruffled
the serenity of the atmosphere, and but few traces of
the storm of the preceding night were visible.

Dr. Rox wished the marshman good day, and after
a few remarks about the storm, inquired whither he
was bound in so great a hurry. Fryer explained that
the sails of the flour-mill wanted mending, and that
Beavis, the proprietor, had sent a boy over to summon
him. The doctor expressed a wish to accompany him,
to which the marshman gladly acceded; and they walked
along together across the flat uninteresting country,
which had little indeed to recommend it to one in search
of the picturesque.

At length Dr. Rox asked after the health of Mary,
and Fryer shook his head. She was very bad, he said,
and he thought he had best send for a medical man;

he did not know what to do exactly, but he was very anxious, and should be glad when his job was over, so that he might get back home again.

"Don't you think, my friend," exclaimed the doctor, "that a man in your position is better off without a family than with one? Don't misunderstand me," he added quickly, as he saw a shade of displeasure cross the broad honest features of the marshman; "I am only alluding to the difficulty you already experience in maintaining your wife and yourself. Consider how your expenses will increase when you are a father."

"I don't know about that, sir," answered Fryer bluntly; "God sends the little innocents, and He will help us to keep them. I've no fear of that; and my old age would be a poor and lonely one if I had ne'er a grandchild to dandle on my knee, and no son or daughter to bring me an odd shilling and a bit of 'bacca when my old bones get rusty and I can't work any longer."

"That is a sentimental rather than a philosophical way to look at the question," said the doctor. "Now, suppose I knew any one who would buy your child when you become a father, and take it right away to a good and comfortable home; suppose—"

"It's no good 'supposing,'" interrupted the marshman rather roughly. "If I were a father, as you say, I wouldn't take a million of money for my child. There now—that's me!"

This was uttered in a tone of such decision, that Dr. Rox did not attempt to renew the discussion. He saw that it would be useless. Fryer added something about "the missis crying her eyes out and going downright mad," the cause being, of course, the suppositionary loss of the child; but the doctor laughingly told him he was only trying the depth of his natural affection; and with a skill peculiarly his own turned the conversation into a channel far more agreeable to his honest and straightforward companion.

An hour and a half of brisk walking brought them to the mill. The sails were secured by the machinery being locked inside; two of them were standing perpendicularly, and the other two were in a horizontal position. The topmost of the upright ones was that which the storm had injured, and it was necessary to repair.

About half-way up, a small gallery ran round the mill, and from this Fryer contrived to climb on to the sails and ascend the damaged one, very much as a sailor climbs up the rigging of a ship.

Dr. Rox had slipped into the mill to look about him. There was no work going on and no one was about. Fryer had some rope, a hammer, a knife, and some nails, which were all the tools he required, and he was soon applying himself to his work with his accustomed energy. His position was not a dangerous one, because he was a man of strong nerves and sober habits. There was little risk of his getting dizzy and tumbling headlong to the ground. Should the mill-sails, however, by any accident get loose, then indeed he would be in peril; for within the last hour a faint breeze had sprung up, and as the mill was on an elevated position, it would suffice to set the sails going with such speed as to jerk off any human being perched like a fly upon them.

Fryer had been at work nearly twenty minutes, and was making satisfactory progress, when he suddenly felt a tremor run through the outside framework. This gave him the impression that the wind was rising, and for a moment he did not attach any importance to the peculiar circumstance.

Suddenly he became aware that he was slowly falling.

The earth got nearer and nearer. The sail above him was changing its position with a movement which every instant became quicker and yet more quick.

Then the terrible truth burst upon him.

Some one inside the mill, unconscious that he was on the sail, had set the machinery in motion. Raising his voice, he exclaimed loudly,

"Stop the mill! For God's sake, mind what you are about, within there! I'm on the sail! Stop the mill! I say, stop the mill!"

No one paid the slightest attention to what he said. It appeared to him that there was no one within hearing; a horrible sensation took possession of him, he became sick and ill, a faintness oppressed him, and his head went dizzy. Clinging like a vice to the sail he held on, still shouting to those whom he supposed to be inside, to stop the mill.

The wind caught up his voice, and returned it to him with a weird mocking echo; and all this time the velocity increased, a whirring noise commenced, and the clanking of the machinery was heard.

Fryer knew that now it was but a question of time. If no one came to his assistance and stopped the mill, he must die. His time on earth was short, for he must infallibly be dashed to pieces.

His loud voice sank to a piteous wail, scarcely audible, and he sobbed in an agony of terror with the hysterical violence of a woman.

Where was Dr. Rox all this time?

Almost as soon as the machinery was put in motion

he had quitted the mill, and walked quickly away across the country. His pace increased, as did the revolution of the sails, and he was soon out of hearing of Fryer's frantic yells for help, which did not come to him.

He was whirled round and round with increasing velocity, and his head became so confused that he could neither see nor think of anything. Yet he clung to the sail, his strength ebbing every minute.

Roused by the unusual spectacle of the mill-sails going round in his absence, the miller Beavis, who was working in a potato-patch he called his garden, rushed up to ascertain the meaning of what he witnessed from afar. As he arrived a heavy substance was whirled through the air, and fell almost at his feet. Starting back in horror and affright, he beheld the body of a man, over which he stooped, recognising in the distorted countenance the well-known features of Fryer, whom he had sent for to mend the broken sail.

The poor wretch had fallen on his head, a slight examination showed that he had broken his neck. Taking up a sack which was lying hard by, the miller threw it over the body and went in search of his men, who were scattered about in various directions, most of them running to the mill, because, to their surprise, they saw the sails were in motion.

The mill was deserted.

No one had seen Fryer arrive, and none knew that he had been accompanied by the doctor, who was by this time out of sight. It was impossible to tell how the machinery had been set going. Perhaps it had not been securely hitched, and some accidental jerk had put it in action.

The idea of any malevolent creature turning on the

machinery was not entertained by any one. Fryer was a good-tempered, amiable fellow, who had never made an enemy in his life. No one owed him a grudge; and while all bewailed the accident, none thought it was anything else.

During this time Dr. Rox made his way to the marsh mill, where Fryer's wife was anxiously waiting her husband's return. She was dangerously ill, and the doctor arrived just in time to find her the mother of a fine boy. It was rash and inconsiderate of him, at such a moment, to tell her of her husband's death; but he did so, and she was instantly seized with convulsions, and became delirious.

His medical knowledge enabled him to see that he had administered a blow from which she would never rally; and with inhuman cruelty he left her to her fate, without endeavouring to alleviate her misery or save her life. Bearing the child in his arms, carefully wrapped up, he again walked briskly across the country.

A few hours later Dr. Rox entered the little insignificant seaside place in which Lady Agneta Evander was staying. She was in her bedroom, having complained of indisposition for the past three days. At the time her indisposition commenced she had received a letter from the doctor couched in obscure terms, but which led her to expect a visit from him at any moment, though no definite period was fixed. Whether this communication had anything to do with her alleged illness or not, we do not pretend to say.

Announcing himself as a doctor, he was ushered by the servant to the apartment occupied by Lady Evander. Under his arm he carried a bundle, but no one knew what it contained.

For two hours Dr. Rox was closeted with Lady Evander; at the expiration of that time he emerged with a grave face, and in an excited manner called to the landlady of the lodging-house.

To her he spoke hurriedly, requesting her to send for a nurse, as her ladyship's condition was critical, and instantly returned to the bedroom.

The next morning Mr. Bellamy received a letter, written and signed by Dr. Rox, a person with whom he was unacquainted, but who was described in the *Medical List*, as he found on reference, as a member of the College of Surgeons, England. This letter informed him that Lady Agneta Evander had been, by him, safely delivered of a son and heir, in the afternoon of the previous day, in the fishing-village of Shingle-cum-Sand in the county of Norfolk, requesting him to communicate the fact to whom it might concern. The doctor's signature followed an announcement to the effect that her ladyship was in good health, and that, in fact, mother and child might be said to be doing well.

This news was of such an important character, that Mr. Bellamy had a horse saddled immediately, and went promptly off to the Moat, where Sir George Evander had established himself, and had already made himself known as a patron of fox-hunting, coursing, badger-baiting, and other manly sports.

Mr. Bellamy having been suspected by the new baronet of sympathising rather too deeply with the enemy, that is to say with Lady Evander, had been dismissed by him from the rather lucrative post of family lawyer, which fact made his present visit and business all the more agreeable to him; for though not a man of a vindictive disposition, he yet had the feelings

D

of a man, and could enjoy turning the tables and paying off an old score.

"Good-morning, Mr. Evander," he said, purposely
omitting the title, as he was ushered into his presence;
"I trust I find you well."

"Please to remember, Mr. Lawyer," answered the
baronet, "that I have my rank—I am Sir George in
the baronetage of the United Kingdom—and I will neither permit a personal slight, nor suffer an unintentional
neglect to pass without notice."

"Very proper, Mr. Evander, if you were right in
your facts," returned Mr. Bellamy.

"What do you mean, sir?" demanded Sir George,
turning pale, as if he imagined he was about to hear
some bad news.

With a cruel and somewhat malicious smile, Mr.
Bellamy explained: "I have to inform you that Lady
Evander yesterday became the mother of a son and
heir. The late Sir Harold has been dead only four
months, therefore—"

"Your informant, sir!" thundered the unfortunate
man, whose hopes were thus all shattered at a single
blow.

"Is the physician who attended her ladyship during
her confinement, and here is his letter. I should advise
you not to contest the matter," added Mr. Bellamy,
"for everything seems plain enough. If you have any
doubt, send an agent down to Shingle-cum-Sand. I shall
proceed there myself in a few hours to wait upon her
ladyship, and will take care that she is not made the
victim of foul play."

This speech was accompanied by a significant glance
at Mr. Evander—Sir George no longer—who was furi-

ous ; but he had sufficient prudence to control his temper, and said quietly, "You can do as you please, sir; but I must request you to get out of this house; for, by the Lord Harry, it will not hold both of us just at this moment."

Mr. Bellamy smiled again, and said, "There is the Aggravated Assaults Act, under which a conviction, without the option of a fine, can be obtained; then there is one's remedy at common law, by means of an action for assault and battery, which results in solid damages. However, I shall make allowance for your feelings, Mr. Evander, and wish you a very good-morning."

He left his former client in a most unenviable state of mind. The poor man was a coward at heart, though a blustering bully. He had a horror of law, of which he knew little, and the course he adopted under the circumstances was this: he had an independent income of five hundred a-year, so that the reverse of fortune did not reduce him to penury or anything like it. During his occupation of the Moat he had spent large sums of money in plate and jewelry, and he had a considerable sum, amounting to a few thousands, in a local bank. He drew this out, and sent his valet down to Shingle-cum-Sand to ascertain the truth of the report of her ladyship's confinement; and while he was gone he packed up the plate and jewelry, as well as his wardrobe, holding himself ready for abdication.

The valet returned, saying that every facility for pursuing his investigations had been given him by Lady Evander, Dr. Rox, and Mr. Bellamy; he had seen and touched the baby, which was shown to him unreservedly.

On hearing this Mr. George Evander wrote a brief

note to her ladyship, the contents of which were as civil as might be expected under the circumstances, and intimated his intention to give her undisputed possession.

In four-and-twenty hours he was in Paris with his money and his jewelry.

Three weeks elapsed, and then Lady Evander arrived at the Moat, accompanied by her physician Dr. Rox, with whose attendance she would not yet dispense, and a nurse engaged at Shingle-cum-Sand, on account of her gross stupidity and general want of intelligence, who carried the infant baronet.

The child was in time christened Charles. Lady Evander had always detested her husband, and would not allow the child to perpetuate his Christian name.

When Lady Evander was properly installed as the mistress of the Moat once more, and all her old friends had called to congratulate her and look at the baby, Dr. Rox thought it time to take his leave.

" All is well now," he said; " no one suspects anything. Remember our compact. The boy will be what you make him, and I ask you to render him as utterly selfish, heartless, and unprincipled as you are yourself, or as I am. Let him go to Eton and Oxford, and when he is of age, expect to see me again. I am going abroad, and I shall pay visits, on and off, to the Palmerston Hotel, Rio Janeiro, in the Brazils, during the next five years, where a letter will find me. Adieu!"

With this speech the mysterious doctor, having finished his work, went away. In the train he had a country newspaper, which gave an account of the melancholy death of a marshman and his wife, on the same day, in the fen districts.

"Such is life!" muttered Dr. Rox; and closing the paper, he shut his eyes and went to sleep.

CHAPTER IV.

THE VIPER ON THE HEARTH.

Dr. Rox's fraud was so successful, that the legitimacy of Lady Evander's son was not suspected for a moment, even by those most affected by the cheat which had been practised upon them.

A gap of twenty years now takes place in our story, during the greater portion of which time her ladyship lived in retirement at Brighton, going little into society, though her well-known face and figure were constantly to be seen at public concerts and on the Parade.

The young baronet grew up, and was, as we have said, christened Charles. From his earliest years he evinced a wayward disposition, and showed an impatience of control. He was educated at a public school and a university, but did not stay long at the latter, being dismissed for some flagrant breach of the college-rules.

Sir Charles Evander speedily made himself known in London, and was the leader of fashionable society. His manner was agreeable, his person charming, and his intellect above the average, but he had no heart. He was cold, callous, and selfish. With ladies he was, nevertheless, very popular, and at an age when most men are first beginning life he was one of the men chiefly talked about in London and Paris.

He was very shrewd in all affairs which had to do

with money, and although he was extravagant to a degree, he had no debts which he could not easily discharge. He played high, and nearly always won. His equipages were the best in the Park, and in dressing he was unrivalled.

Before we introduce the young baronet to the reader, we must pay a visit to an ancient country house, the property of Lord Carisbrook, who was seldom tempted to visit London. At an early age he had married his cousin Emily. It was purely a love match, and their union had been productive of unadulterated happiness to both of them.

On a fine day in the autumn of the year, Lord and Lady Carisbrook were seated under the shade of a spreading beech-tree in the gardens attached to Caldecott Hall, which was the name of their ancestral abode. His lordship was reading a letter he had received from his brother in London, and when he had completed its perusal, he exclaimed:

"Hubert says in his letter, my dear, that he has dispatched to us Sir Charles Evander, a young baronet of whom I have heard something. He is a friend of Hubert's, who knows his mother very well, and he wishes him to be kept for some time in the country, if possible, as the delights of London are rapidly demoralising him."

"I shall be glad to extend our hospitality to any friend of your brother Hubert's," answered Lady Carisbrook, who rarely contradicted her husband in anything.

"The letter goes on to say," continued his lordship, "that Lady Evander wishes him to renew his acquaintance with the St. Aubyns, who live near us. Sir Charles and Lily St. Aubyn met in town; and if a match could be arranged between them, it would be most desirable."

"We will do what we can," said her ladyship, favouring her husband with a sweet smile. "I am sure we have been so happy during our wedded life, dearest Albert, that we need have no compunction in inducing two young people to unite themselves together."

After some further conversation it was decided that they would gladly receive Sir Charles Evander as a guest, and do all they could to make him forget the delights of the town by introducing to his notice the many charms of a country life.

During the remainder of the evening Lord Carisbrook was grave and silent. There was something so unusual about this, that his wife could not refrain from asking him the cause of his sudden melancholy.

With a sigh, he said:

"I was reading a book this morning, in which the author lays down the curious doctrine that people can be too happy, and he adds that a long continuation of happiness is sure to be followed by some calamity."

"Well," said Lady Carisbrook, "what has that to do with us? It seems to me that your author is very eccentric. I should discard such reading."

"It has everything to do with us, my dear," answered his lordship. "We have been married five years, we are both young, and we have enjoyed uninterrupted happiness during our wedded life. If the author is correct in his theory, I fear that the time is approaching for some desperate calamity to befall us."

"You are nervous and low-spirited to-night, Albert," exclaimed Lady Carisbrook, in a tone of deep concern. "Pray let us talk about something else. I am convinced that your author is a man upon whom no reliance can be placed."

Lord Carisbook sighed again, and he talked indifferently on various subjects, though his thoughts ran in the same groove, as he was unable to divest himself of the superstitious terror with which a dread of coming evil had filled him.

It seemed to him that the arrival of Sir Charles Evander would, in some mysterious way, be connected with the misfortunes which he anticipated, and he had considerable difficulty in writing the letter which gave his consent to the visit.

A week elapsed, and Sir Charles Evander arrived at Caldecott Hall.

He was tall, handsome, well-made, and had that indescribable, easy, well-bred air which can only be acquired from moving in the best society. There was magic in his eyes, and Lady Carisbrook had not been in his company half an hour, before she felt fascinated by his glance, and turning away with a shudder, said to herself:

"That is indeed a man for a woman to love. How happy should Miss St. Aubyn be with such a suitor!"

Sir Charles Evander could talk well; he also knew when to listen, and never monopolised the conversation. He had a fund of anecdote at his fingers' ends; was never at a loss for a joke; and though sometimes severe in his criticism on women, he was nevertheless often their champion on various points.

Young as he was, he had seen a great deal of the world, which had made him somewhat of a cynic. In reality he dazzled, rather than made a real impression on his friends, for there was nothing genuine or sincere about him. He turned everything into ridicule, and laughed at everybody.

Carisbrook soon discovered that he was an accomplished sportsman, and that the amusements of the city had not rendered him in any way effeminate.

They went out together on shooting expeditions, and always came back with full bags, Sir Charles being an excellent shot, and thoroughly at home with dog and gun.

There were so many places on the estate to go to, so much to see, and so much to do during Sir Charles Evander's first week at Caldecott, that Lady St. Aubyn was forgotten.

At length Lady Carisbrook exclaimed, "We have some most agreeable neighbours, Sir Charles, to whom I shall feel delighted to introduce you. Among others, I may mention the St. Aubyns."

"Of Rock Hill?" said Sir Charles. "Yes, I have met them, and shall be glad to renew the acquaintance. Lily is a fine girl, and she assisted me to pass some time very pleasantly in London."

"We will invite them to meet you at dinner, Sir Charles," exclaimed Lady Carisbrook; "but you must not suppose that we have any design upon your heart in bringing you in contact with the most lovely young lady in the county."

Sir Charles Evander laughed, and made answer, "I do not think I am so impressionable as you seem to imagine, although I will own myself susceptible of a woman's charms."

Presently Lord Carisbrook went to the other end of the room, and Evander had an opportunity of saying in a low tone,

"My heart is gone already, Lady Carisbrook."

"Indeed! Since when, may I ask?" she replied, with a slight elevation of the eyebrows.

"Since I entered this house; since I first beheld you, Lady Carisbrook," he said, with a glance of admiration.

"Sir Charles," exclaimed her ladyship, in a tone of severe rebuke, "if you dare to repeat such language to me, I shall instantly make my husband acquainted with your conduct. You, a guest in his house, and to make such a speech to the wife of your host!"

"Why not, when the hostess is pretty?" answered Evander, twirling his moustache.

Lady Carisbrook half rose, as if to call her husband's attention; but he was looking over some books, and had his back turned towards her.

"If you wish to lose your husband, by all means promote a quarrel between us," said Sir Charles coolly. "Duelling is possible in France, and I can fire a pistol with as much skill as I can use a sword."

She became passive under this threat, and again his large lustrous eyes were fixed upon her, appearing to fathom the secret depths of the innermost recesses of her soul.

Lady Carisbrook began to be afraid of this man: but after his familiarity that evening, she always avoided a conversation with him.

Was her husband's instinct right, and was this young man to come between them like a cloud, obscuring the happiness which had hitherto brightened their domestic horizon?

She breathed a fervent prayer that it might not be so.

A few days afterwards Lord Carisbrook and Sir Charles Evander were out shooting together near the confines of the estate. By their side was the main road, and they sat down upon a bank to rest, while the keepers spread a slight repast they had brought with them.

Suddenly the noise of horses galloping rapidly along the road fell upon their ears; with this was mingled the clatter of wheels and the cries of women, apparently in a dreadful state of alarm.

Sir Charles Evander was up in a moment, looking eagerly along the highway.

Presently he beheld a carriage drawn by two fiery horses, over which the terrified coachman had lost all control, descending a hill at a rapid pace. In the carriage, which was enveloped in a cloud of dust, he was able to distinguish two ladies. Their danger was imminent; for a few yards farther on was a curve in the road, round which it seemed impossible for the horses to turn without upsetting the carriage, an accidental occurrence which might cost the inmates their lives.

Without a moment's hesitation Sir Charles Evander shouldered his gun, and taking aim at the nearest of the maddened horses, waited until it came within range, and fired.

So successful was the shot, that the animal dropped down dead at once. Its companion tore along a few feet farther, but, hampered with the weight of the body, could not make way, and was pulled up panting and trembling by the driver, who was overjoyed to be so easily and unexpectedly extricated from the peril in which his careless driving had placed himself and the ladies.

Vaulting lightly over a gate, Sir Charles was quickly on the spot. He found two ladies in the carriage, which was not in the least damaged. They were inclined to faint, but, recovering themselves at the sight of their preserver, their eyes beamed gratitude upon him. To his delight Sir Charles Evander recognised Mrs. St. Aubyn and her daughter Lily, to whose peerless face a deep flush lent additional beauty and charms.

Lord Carisbrook was on the scene almost as soon as Sir Charles, and exclaimed, while the latter was bowing politely to Lily St. Aubyn,

"I sincerely trust you are uninjured?"

"O, thank you both very much," answered Mrs. St. Aubyn, in a voice that trembled a little; "we have escaped with a fright and a slight shaking; though, had it not been for Sir Charles Evander's skill and presence of mind, I shudder to think what our fate might have been."

"You overrate my poor service," said Sir Charles. "Perhaps you will not believe me when I say that I took almost as much pleasure in killing your horse as I experienced in saving you."

"O, Sir Charles," said Lily, "you always take such delight in depreciating yourself."

"Do I?" he replied, with a laugh. "Set it down, then, to my innate modesty. Candidly, however, I am very glad to think that no harm has happened to you."

"We intended calling at Rock Hill to pay our respects to you, Mrs. St. Aubyn, any time for the last week," exclaimed Lord Carisbrook.

"You honour us too greatly, my lord," she replied.

"It is you who confer the honour upon those whom

you are gracious enough to receive," said his lordship, with a low bow; adding, "Can I ask you to walk over to Caldecott? You cannot proceed with one horse, and my man shall drive you home later in the day."

"I accept your offer with pleasure," rejoined Mrs. St. Aubyn. "Are we far from the Hall?"

"A mile and a half will cover the distance. Come, let me give you my arm, and Evander will escort your daughter."

The gentlemen handed their guns to the keepers, who had already opened the gate to allow the ladies to pass through, and the little party started across the fields in the direction of Caldecott Hall.

Sir Charles Evander found the walk very agreeable to him. He allowed Lord Carisbrook and Mrs. St. Aubyn to take the lead, and he had undisturbed possession of Lily, who was equally delighted to be alone with him.

She had fallen in love with him in London during the season, but had tried to persuade herself that it was a mere girlish fancy, as he had not paid her any particular attention—certainly not enough for her to build any extravagant expectations on.

His present amiability and fondness seemed a confirmation of all her dearest hopes and most secret aspirations.

Evander was growing tired of sporting. Flirting was necessary to his existence, and the severe virtue of Lady Carisbrook did not at present give him much encouragement in that quarter. The season was over, every one was out of town, and the hope of meeting Lily St. Aubyn was the only thing which had prevented him taking his leave of the kind and hospitable occupiers of Caldecott Hall, and seeking such diversion as the capitals of the Continent or the German watering-places could afford.

"Until I met you, Miss St. Aubyn," he said, pressing her hand, "I was like a man wandering in a land where the sun never shines."

"And now?"—she paused with an arch smile.

"Now I am in paradise," he said gallantly.

When they reached Caldecott Hall, the blushing girl who was hanging on his arm at once attracted Lady Carisbrook's notice.

A pang shot through her heart.

"What," she exclaimed to herself, "am I jealous? O, it is absolutely necessary for my peace of mind that that man should leave this house."

CHAPTER V

A COMPROMISING LETTER.

THE pleasant party at Caldecott Hall was soon broken up. The St. Aubyns returned to town; and Sir Charles Evander, growing tired of the country and its amusements, made his excuses to Lord and Lady Carisbrook, and also sought the gay metropolis. Her ladyship felt very dull and miserable when the young baronet had taken his departure. In vain she struggled with her melancholy, and asked her wayward heart what Sir Charles could possibly be to her. But the witty and vivacious young man, with all his cynicism, had made an impression upon her which she found it impossible to throw off. Formerly she had found pleasure in her home duties and her husband's society. Now she called her life tedious, and sighed for excitement which she could not have in the solitude of the country.

It was not that Lord Carisbrook was less kind and loving to her. He was as attentive as ever; more so, in fact, when he saw that her spirits drooped, and that she lacked her sprightly air, produced by a genuine happiness and content which had formerly characterised all her actions.

She longed, also, to go to town, and soon made her husband acquainted with her wishes. He was so satisfied with his country home, and the sports he there enjoyed, that he combated the resolution. She, with the obstinacy of a woman firmly resolved upon adopting a particular course, listened in sullen silence to his arguments, and sighed when she ought to have smiled, casting a chill over his heart, and clouding that domestic felicity which he had before regarded as so perfect.

"I cannot account for this sudden change in your tastes, my dear," he said, when she had for the fiftieth time contrasted the delights of the city with the dulness of which she was the unwilling victim in the country. "Here you have the society of agreeable neighbours. I am always with you; and your wishes are gratified as soon as made. In London you will have the worry of a thousand parties, balls, and theatres. The bloom which now glows on your cheek will be exchanged for an unhealthy pallor; and we shall increase our expenses by at least a third."

"O, if it is a matter of money, and you wish to be a

miser, that is another thing, and I shall say no more,"
answered Lady Carisbrook. "I always thought that
we were sufficiently rich to be able to take our proper
place in society, and I fondly supposed that you were
retrenching at Caldecott in order that we might some
day shine in the most brilliant circle in town. I did
not know that when I married I renounced the delights
of the world, and was to be shut up in this dismal bar-
rack-like place."

Here she sighed more profoundly than she had done
before, her languid eyes cast down in a melancholy
fashion. She watched her husband through their long
fringes, and was pleased to perceive that her words had
produced an effect upon him.

He paced restlessly up and down the apartment,
and at length stopped in front of her with his hands in
his pockets.

"If you have made up your mind to go, Emily," he
said, "I suppose I might, like Canute, as well try to
stem the tide as to keep you here; but I must say that
you are not the dutiful and obedient wife I have hitherto
found you. Our happiness is not a thing of yesterday,
and I was right when I feared that it was too perfect to
last. I know very well what the dissipations and dis-
tractions of a town life are. Your time will never be
your own, and we shall no longer be able to enjoy our
own society as we have done. You will have to attend
balls and parties, receive visitors, and return calls. You
will be the veriest slave in existence; and the only
relief I shall have will be a chat at the club, attendance at some theatre, or an occasional pigeon-shooting
match in the environs of London—a pleasant prospect,
truly!"

"That speech," said Lady Carisbrook, who saw the commanding position it gave her, "sufficiently proves the selfishness of your nature. I must be sacrificed, because you want to indulge your brutal instinct of killing something. If you have not your gun or your fishing-rod in your hand, you are not happy, and when those pursuits fail you, a horse and dogs enable you to chase a poor fox to death, or cruelly mangle an inoffensive hare. Have you no intellect—no fancy for politics? A seat in the House of Commons is worthy of a man's ambition; and if you could get returned for some borough or county, your position would increase my power."

"No, thank you," he replied; "I am not inclined to falsify the example of a third of a lifetime to gratify your newly-born ambition. No politics for me. I will humour you so far as to take you to town, on the understanding that, if I let you please yourself, you will not interfere with me; and I pray most devoutly that you will soon get tired of your career of folly, for the pursuit of fashion is nothing better."

"Thank you for your tardy compliance," rejoined Lady Carisbrook, whose face exhibited a flush of triumph and pleasure which she could not repress; "I could have wished, though, that you had yielded more gracefully."

"Women are difficult to please," he said, with a gesture of annoyance; "I flattered myself that my wife was superior to the ordinary run, but I am mistaken. I must have been blind to have deceived myself so long. No matter. My eyes are open now, and I shall in future be able to estimate you at your true value, Emily."

"Here is a torrent of abuse for daring to call my

E

soul my own, and making an effort to escape from the house of bondage!" cried her ladyship with a laugh.

Lord Carisbrook did not condescend to reply. He walked with long strides into the hall, put on his hat, took up his gun, and going into the yard, whistled a couple of dogs to his feet, and started for the woods to vent his spleen upon the unsuspecting pheasants.

Lady Carisbrook had gained her point. Caldecott was shut up, and the servants sent to town to a house which his lordship's agent had taken for them, ready furnished for occupation, in a fashionable part of the West-end. It was in Wilton-crescent, and they were not far from Hans-place, where the St. Aubyns resided.

Her ladyship did not much care about them, because she fancied that Sir Charles Evander paid the lovely Lily too much attention; but she was obliged to keep on friendly terms with them, because they were invited everywhere, and she would meet them at all good houses.

Sir Charles was soon made aware of Lady Carisbrook's presence in town, and he laughed in his sleeve, for he knew enough of women and their characters to understand that as he had gone away from her, she had followed him. He had never entertained a doubt that he would have an opportunity of completing the conquest he had commenced at Caldecott; and he resolved to devote his leisure moments to the beautiful Emily, whose husband was still confiding enough to believe that her heart was yet as thoroughly his own as it had been in the happy days of yore.

The gentlemen whom Lady Carisbrook met, and to whom she talked about Sir Charles, did not give Evander the best possible character. These were two friends of his, Captain Vavasour and Mr. Frederick Mordaunt, the latter of whom was constantly at the St. Aubyns', and at all places where he thought he should meet Lily and this conduct of his was not at all surprising, for he loved her passionately, though she had not in any marked measure encouraged the preference which he exhibited for her.

Both the Captain and Mr. Mordaunt, though associating with Sir Charles Evander at clubs and other places, did not think themselves under an obligation to speak well of him or defend his character, and the hints which they threw out respecting his licentiousness and want of principle should have put her ladyship on her guard; but it did no such thing.

She was pleased that such a gay Lothario should evince a decided preference for her, and his charms in her eyes were increased by the fact that he was a general and successful admirer of the fair sex.

Mr. Mordaunt had taken a strong dislike to Sir Charles Evander ever since he first met him at Hans-place. The attitude which the latter assumed towards Lily convinced the jealous mind of the lover that he was in love with her, and that she did not object to his admiration. Mordaunt's affection for her was so sincere, that if he could not win her himself, he wished to see her married to one who would insure her happiness, and this he felt certain Sir Charles would not do. He could say nothing to either Lily or her mother, because they would accuse him of an interested motive in vilifying a man he had treated as his friend.

To Lady Carisbrook, however, he was not so reticent. He told her his opinion of the baronet, though there was no tinge of acrimony or malice in what he said. He spoke his mind freely, with the air of one who was fearless of the consequences, and knew that he was uttering the truth. Lady Carisbrook had invited this confidence on the part of Mr. Mordaunt and Captain Vavasour; but when she had gained it, she was displeased with them for running down one whom she liked, and on one occasion said with some asperity,

"If Sir Charles Evander is such as you describe him to be, I wonder that you associate with him."

"For my part," replied Mr. Mordaunt, "I can answer that I have for some time ceased to do so. I am coldly civil whenever we meet, and he must know that I do not class him among the number of my friends."

"That must be a great deprivation for Sir Charles. What do you say, Captain Vavasour?" said her ladyship.

Frederick Mordaunt was grieved, but did not retort; he seemed to await his friend's reply with some anxiety.

"I cannot say that I admire Evander's principle," answered Vavasour: "but I like the man, and am still his friend. I tell him to his face what I say behind his back; and he laughs at me, telling me that I am a child in the ways of the world, and will know better some day. I do not agree with him; for I can never believe that it is right to trifle with the affections of a woman—her trust, confidence, and weakness should be her protection."

"Admirably spoken," exclaimed Lady Carisbrook. "I honour you for the expression of such sentiments, and am inclined to think that your friend is only young and thoughtless, and that he will learn wisdom shortly. In the mean time I shall not close my door against him; for one might exclude many agreeable acquaintances, if any blot upon one's moral character were to be an insuperable bar against admission to a London drawing-room. If we are truly charitable, we should be blind to each other's faults."

Mordaunt shook his head and walked away. Captain Vavasour was inclined to agree with her ladyship; and they changed the conversation, the latter saying,

"We shall meet to-morrow evening, I presume, at Hans-place. All the world will be at Mrs. St. Aubyn's reception, and as I have so few friends in town, I shall be glad to see a face I know. Lord Carisbrook leaves London for a week to-morrow morning, to see after his poor dogs and horses, about whom he frets so much. Was it not cruel of me to separate them?"

"On the contrary, I, for one, can only esteem myself fortunate that you refused to any longer shut so much beauty up in the seclusion of a country house," replied the Captain gallantly.

"O, Captain Vavasour!" cried Lady Carisbrook. "You army men have such an agreeable way of flattering, that I do not wonder you are popular with the ladies."

The Captain smiled and twirled his moustache, and after about ten minutes' more small-talk, he quitted the house with Mr. Mordaunt, and went to another house not far off to pay a fresh call.

The party given by Mrs. St. Aubyn, to which her ladyship had alluded, was merely a reception. Visitors dropped in as they liked, went from group to group, chatting first with one, then with another, and took their departure when it pleased them without any ceremony. It is true there was a card-room for those who liked a serious, business-like evening, and there were singing and playing in the back drawing-room, while refreshments were provided in a separate apartment downstairs.

Lady Carisbrook made her appearance about ten o'clock, superbly dressed, and almost the first person she met on entering, after having spoken to her amiable hostess, was Sir Charles Evander, whom she thought had never looked handsomer. Evening-dress became him wonderfully well, and he was always perfectly dressed.

"This is kind of you," he exclaimed. "There is no one worth speaking to here, and I was getting awfully bored. Lord Melvern and I were thinking of leaving, but the hope that you might yet appear sustained me for thirty dismal weary minutes. May I inquire where Carisbrook is?"

"Did you not know that he had left town?" she replied, showing her pearly teeth and fluttering her fan. "I am quite alone. Dogs and horses have superior attractions, and he has gone back to Caldecott. I do not know what I shall do with myself."

"I am acquainted with married women," answered Sir Charles, twisting his moustache, "who would not consider such an occurrence a calamity. They would be glad of a little relief from the presence of their lord and master."

"That is charming," said Emily eagerly. "You are just the man I wanted to meet. I have never been separated from my husband before for a single day, and I have been in despair to discover some means of passing the time. You say that you know ladies who have been similarly situated. You will tell me what they did, will you not? Please, do take compassion upon me and tell me."

"With the greatest pleasure," rejoined Sir Charles Evander. "I must premise, however, that my ladies were not of the sentimental order. They did not look upon husbands generally as an unqualified good, and they enjoyed their freedom by such innocent little amusements as giving dinner-parties to an intimate friend or friends. I have had such an invitation myself; a box at the theatre has diversified the proceedings."

"Excellent!" exclaimed Lady Carisbrook; "I am sure that I cannot do better than follow such a capital example. Will you favour me with your company at my house to dinner to-morrow at seven, Sir Charles?"

"I shall be most happy," he said.

Lily St. Aubyn came up, and they were separated; but Lady Carisbrook had made the engagement, calculating upon her husband's absence, without meaning any harm, though she ought to have known it was wrong to do anything which she could not tell his lordship.

The early part of the day was passed by her in buying flowers in Covent-garden, and making preparations for a charming little dinner, such as would at once display her taste and the resources of her establishment.

In the afternoon she went to her bedroom to lie down and rest for an hour. She was tired. It had been quite late when she left the St. Aubyns', and not used to such hours, she found it difficult to recover from the fatigue which they occasioned.

To her surprise she was disturbed, as she was about to close her eyes for a refreshing sleep, by a knocking at the door.

"It is only me, Emily," said a voice, which she recognised instantly.

"Good gracious, my husband! What brings him back? Can he suspect?" she began, when her speculations were cut short by the entrance of Lord Carisbrook, who caught her in his arms, and kissing her tenderly, cried:

"Here I am again, dearest, sooner than you expected. Ah, what is this? You do not seem so pleased to see me as I thought you would be!"

"You frightened me. I was half asleep, and my nerves are a little weak. I was at Mrs. St. Aubyn's last night till late," she answered, rubbing her eyes, and sitting on the edge of the bed, wrapped as she was in the capacious folds of a pink dressing-gown.

"I knew dissipation would knock you up, and I am not sorry to see that I was not mistaken in my anticipation. But do you not want to hear what has brought me away from Caldecott in such a hurry, when I had resolved to stay there for a week?"

"I am a little curious, I must confess," said Emily, who was dying with curiosity, but did not like to ask any questions.

"A relative of mine, who made a fortune in India, became eccentric, and lived in London under another name, goodness knows why. He is dead—died yesterday, in fact—and his solicitor has written to me to say that he has left me the greater portion of his wealth."

"There is nothing very interesting about that," her ladyship said. "We have as much money as we want already. Is that all that has brought you up in such a hurry? As for me, I would not have gone across the street for such news."

" You have very strange ideas !" replied Lord Carisbrook, with a tone of disappointment. " You were sorry
at seeing me, and now you don't care for the legacy.
I look forward to buying you a set of diamonds. I can
build some more stables at Caldecott, and I shall be
able to hunt the country, which I could not do before.
I have already settled the site of the kennels."

" If you are pleased, it does not matter to me one
way or the other," she said with a half yawn. " I do
like people to be exact and consistent, though. Your
return has destroyed my projects of independence for a
week. I was going out to dinner to-night, and—"

" What is to prevent you ?" interrupted Carisbrook.
" I have engaged myself to the solicitor, and shall very
likely stay late talking over matters with him. I shall
not be home till twelve certainly ; so you can go where
you like, without paying the slightest attention to me."

" On that understanding I congratulate you," exclaimed her ladyship ; "and now please go away and
leave me. I am dying for rest, and must have some.
I shall be good for nothing, else."

Imprinting another kiss upon her lips, Lord Carisbrook took his departure, called a cab, drove to his
club, told his friends of his good fortune, and ordered
dinner ; going back to dress, and returning in time to
meet the solicitor, who was going to dine with him, and
not he with the man of law, as he had said. So there
was a little harmless deception on his side.

Her ladyship determined to be brave, and receive
Sir Charles Evander, though prudence dictated the
adoption of a very different course. A letter would
have put him off, but she would not write a line which
would deprive her of her anticipated pleasure. She

knew it was wrong to have Sir Charles at her house, and it was for that very reason she made up her mind to do it.

It happened that Sir Charles Evander was more considerate. He belonged to the same club as Lord Carisbrook, and met him there in the afternoon.

"How do?" he exclaimed. "I thought you a hundred miles away in the country."

"At Caldecott," replied his lordship. "I have only just returned. Business brought me back. It was a great pity. I never saw finer weather for shooting."

Sir Charles went to the writing-room, and wrote a letter to Emily, in which he said that he had seen her husband, and hoped she would, under these circumstances, excuse him for breaking his appointment, as he had no wish to meet Carisbrook. He sincerely trusted that this evening alone was only a pleasure deferred.

In the hall he did not see Carisbrook, who was putting on his hat, and he said to the porter distinctly in his lordship's hearing:

"Give this letter to a commissionnaire, and let him take it to Lady Carisbrook's, Wilton-crescent."

These words fell like a thunderbolt upon his lordship, who, half-stupefied, watched Sir Charles reënter the club. He was himself going for a stroll round St. James's-square, in which his club was situated, to get an appetite for dinner; and changing his mind, he put down his hat, and extended his hand to the porter, and said:

"Give me that letter; it's for my wife, and I can deliver it. Most probably Sir Charles Evander did not see me, or he would have asked me to take charge of it."

The porter did as he was requested, thinking there was no harm in complying with such a request; and Lord Carisbrook, fuming like an angry lion, went upstairs to the smoking-room to read the letter at his leisure, unobserved and uninterrupted.

Its contents astounded him. They, indeed, were calculated to throw suspicion upon the conduct of any woman; and if a man had plunged a knife into his heart, he would not have felt more exquisite pain than he did in reading this compromising letter of Sir Charles Evander's.

"This is terrible!" he muttered, wiping the perspiration, which had gathered on his brow in great drops, away with his hand. "No wonder Emily was not anxious to see me. This is how she enjoys her independence. But the affair cannot rest here. It was, indeed, an unlucky day for me when Sir Charles Evander crossed my threshold. Bitterly shall he repent his treachery. I must kill that man, or he shall kill me!"

A mist swam before his eyes, and he almost fainted. It was a dreadful blow to him to find his cherished happiness vanishing, like a phantom, into thin air.

CHAPTER VI.

A SCENE ON THE PARADE.

FINDING that Lord Carisbrook had unexpectedly returned to "spoil sport," as he expressed himself, Sir Charles Evander went off to Brighton that evening, to keep an appointment which he had previously made.

It was the season at that fashionable watering-place ; and as he walked on the Parade and the new pier on the morning after his arrival, he met a constant succession of friends and acquaintances.

There was one, however, among them whom he did not expect to meet, and that was Lord Carisbrook, who, receiving information in town that Evander had taken his departure for Brighton, followed him almost immediately, to demand an explanation of his behaviour to his wife, and especially to ask the meaning of the contents of the letter he had intercepted.

They met face to face on the Parade, nearly opposite the Bedford Hotel, and Lord Carisbrook, who was a very passionate man, endeavoured to speak. His rage, however, deprived him of the power of articulate utterance, and all Evander could distinguish was :

"My wife ! my wife, Sir Charles !"

"Lady Carisbrook was very well when last I had the pleasure of seeing her, and kind even to the verge of affection," answered Evander with a mocking smile.

This reply was well calculated to raise the irascible nobleman's passion to its height, and utterly losing all control over himself, he violently struck Evander on the head with a heavy cane he carried. The force of the blow was sufficient to stun the unfortunate baronet, who would have fallen to the ground, had he not been caught in the arms of a young man who was passing by.

A crowd collected, and Carisbrook walked quickly on, fearful of being arrested by the police for the assault which he had committed : and so alarmed was he that he left Brighton directly, and going on to Dover, went over to France, until the affair should blow over.

Evander was soon recognised by his friends, and

carried to his hotel adjacent, the young man who had first assisted him being with him all the time.

Happily the doctor who was called in pronounced the wound of little consequence, prescribed rest, and took his leave.

When all had gone away but the young man who had assisted him in the first instance, Evander looked up and inquired his name. He was a fine-looking fellow of about nineteen, intelligent as well as handsome.

"I am a namesake of your own, Sir Charles," answered the young man. "I came to Brighton yesterday to see you, as I am in very reduced circumstances, and you are my only relative; my father, Mr. George Evander, being dead. I daresay you know that if your birth had not taken place, I should have succeeded my father in the title and estates, and the world would have seen a Sir Noel Evander instead of Sir Charles."

"I am very weak and ill just now," replied Evander, whose face exhibited a strange pallor, "and I shall esteem it a favour if you will call upon me to-morrow, Mr. Evander. You can then tell me in what way I can be of service to you, and I can make what answer I think fit."

Noel bowed and retired, hopeful that he should meet with that assistance of which he stood in need.

It will be remembered that Mr. George Evander was the heir-at-law of the baronet, who committed suicide, and that he would have been entitled to the estates and the title, had not Dr. Rox been so successful in the fraud which he had perpetrated. As a matter of fact, Charles was a usurper, and that which he enjoyed should have been Noel's.

The latter young man had been very unlucky. His

father had educated him well; but when the time came for him to give him a profession, and start him in the world, the bank in which all his money was placed suspended payment, through the dishonesty of one of the partners, and he, in conjunction with many others, was left without a penny. Therefore he, being destitute, died in a week of a broken heart; and his son, selling what few things remained to him, determined to seek his rich cousin, Sir Charles Evander, and beg a little temporary help from him.

He little knew Evander, who had a horror of poor relations, and resolved, on reflection, to have nothing to do with him. What did it matter to him if he had no means of gaining a livelihood?

When the poor fellow came next day Sir Charles refused to see him, alleging his illness as an excuse; and when Noel Evander called again, he was given a cruel hard note, enclosing five pounds, which was all that the writer—so said the letter—was able, or disposed, to give him.

Noel's necessities were so pressing that he could not refuse the money; but he went away with a sensation of loneliness and desolation which he had not experienced since his father's melancholy death.

Sir Charles soon recovered from the effects of the blow which Lord Carisbrook had given him, and he was amply recompensed for it by the sympathy of his friends and the admiration of the ladies, who all heard that he had been ill-treated for making love. True, it was to another man's wife; but they did not consider that a crime in a man, though they condemned it in the woman; and Lady Carisbrook was looked coldly upon by every one; and her husband kept away

on two grounds. The first was, his fear of a prosecu-
tion for the assault by Evander; and the second, his
firm conviction that his wife was unworthy of his esteem.
So he dragged on a weary existence on the Continent,
having behaved as foolishly as he could, and plunged
into all sorts of excesses, which ruined his health and
drained his purse.

Noel was thoroughly adrift. He had expected some
substantial help from his cousin, and the five pounds
he had received was all, except a few shillings, which
he had in the world. Five pounds? It is not much
to begin the world with; and he wandered along the
Parade and up Market-street to the Western-road, and
on into North-street, turning up a small thoroughfare
in the poorest part of Brighton.

Feeling fatigued, he was about to enter a public-
house, whose magnificent proportions and wealth of
plate-glass arrested his attention, when a voice of distress emanating from a neighbouring alley made him
turn his footsteps in that direction. Passing under an
archway, he entered a yard having a pump in the
centre and doors on either side.

This paradise was known as Eden-gardens.

Eden-gardens! Powers above, what a misnomer!
It is to be hoped that some of the poor creatures living
in that place, called "a grove because there was nothing
shady about it," were deluded by the Edenic name into
believing that they were dwelling in a healthy part,
even if horticulture neglected and omitted did not carry
out the delusion.

At the door of one of the houses a group of people
had collected, consisting of dirty, ill- and scantily-dressed
women, slip-shod, blear-eyed, and dishevelled. *Item*—

men unshaven, grimy, unhealthy, short-pipe-smoking, and decidedly beery: with children at their heels who were the most perfect exemplification of the offspring of gin-drinking, poverty-stricken, improvident parents that could be met with.

The cause of the disturbance was at once apparent. Bailiffs had taken possession of a house numbered nine in Eden-gardens, and were distraining—probably for rent. We may with certainty say for rent, as no one but a landlord would trust any one further than they could see them while living in Eden-gardens, which, spite of its rosy name, did not enjoy the best reputation.

Sundry articles of furniture were dragged out of the house, and placed upon the flags of the court. On the stairs of the house, and impeding the bailiffs in every way, were a woman and three children. A man stood in the court clinging to the furniture, and making pathetic appeals to the neighbours.

This was Pat Rooney—an Irishman, as his name implies. He had been out of luck lately, and fallen in arrear with his landlord, who wanted his rent, and, as he could not get it, distrained for it. As Noel came up, the Irishman said, "O, wirra, wirra, that I should live to see this day! Woe, heavy and bitter woe, betide ye who are doing this! Is it turning me and the colleen and the childre out of house and home into the sthreets for the sake of a little dhirty silver? By the sowls of the dead"—he uttered this oath in Irish—"were ye in Ireland, there would be blood, red blood, shed this night!"

"What is all this about?" exclaimed Noel, addressing nobody in particular.

Every one answered him at once; and it was at

length made clear to his comprehension that Pat Rooney was being distrained on for rent.

"Yes, yer honour," chimed in Rooney: "and all for the palthry sum of four pounds ten shillings, bar one halfpenny! Shure and if me father was alive he'd have paid tin times the sum; but he's dead and gone, and I am far from Ballynahog, or the haythens wouldn't dare to trate me in this whay."

Turning to the bailiff, who at that moment entered the court with a mattress in his arms, Noel said,

"What does this man owe you?"

"Four pounds ten shillings is the figure," replied the bailiff, dropping the mattress, and looking curiously at his questioner.

"Will that pay you out, and satisfy all demands?"

"Well, it will if it comes to that; but me an' me mate 'll expect something for our trouble."

"Then you will expect what you will not get. Here is the sum you demand. Sit down and write a receipt, or else produce the one your employer provided you with."

"Here it is, stamped and all," replied the bailiff, drawing a piece of crumpled paper from his pocket, and biting each sovereign between his teeth as he received it from Noel.

"Are you satisfied?"

"The debt is: but you might stand a drop of beer, guv'nor. It won't break your bank."

Noel gave the man sixpence, who whistled to his companion and went away, not at all sorry that his unpleasant occupation was over.

Pat Rooney was stupefied with surprise, and so was his wife. The children continued to howl with that

F

delightful facility peculiar to the younger sons and daughters of Erin. Suddenly Pat sprang up and caught Noel by the hand, the back of which he kissed. "God bless you now, whoever you are!" he said, in a hearty voice. "By the five crasses, and this is a white day. Rosha darlint, come and thank the gentleman, for he's bought the brokers, bad cess to them! out of the house; and we sha'n't lose our purty home, and the childre won't die in the gutther. Hurroo! More power to his honour's elbow, I say!"

Then followed a curious scene. The Irish family, from the father to the youngest child, crowded round Noel, and nearly tore him to pieces in their well-meant demonstration of joy. After that, other Irish families in the court insisted upon shaking hands "wid his honour," and tears of joy and gratitude fell fast as rain in April.

Noel remarked that Mrs. Patrick Rooney was a tidy, pretty-looking woman, and that her children were neatly and cleanly dressed; so he could easily believe her when she said that they had been unfortunate through Pat's being out of work, owing to an accident.

The neighbours volunteered in a body to help Mrs. Rooney to carry her furniture upstairs to the second floor; and Noel took advantage of the opportunity to give the receipt to the Irishman, and say, "Now that I have obliged you, my friend, I am going to ask you to oblige me."

"Shure, and your honour's self has but to say the word."

"Will you give me a lodging for a short time; for all my money, except a few shillings, I have given to the bailiffs, and I am without a home?"

"Widout a home!" said the Irishman, the tears springing to his eyes as he spoke; "widout a home, and will I give you one? Will I? Is it Pathrick Rooney that will do it? By the seven sisters of mercy, he will, if he sleeps on the stones for it!"

CHAPTER VII.

NOEL BECOMES ACQUAINTED WITH MISS ALMA MAITLAND OF MAITLAND.

THE kind-hearted Irish people did not know how to do enough for Noel. Their delight when they found out that he was not a rich gentleman was a thing to see—we frankly confess that we cannot adequately describe it. Their unbounded pleasure at least showed that their gratitude and offers of assistance to him were, if nothing else, genuine.

At first they had supposed him a rich and charitable man seeking opportunities of doing good, and never neglecting them; when they discovered that he was like themselves poor and in want, they redoubled their courtesies, wanting to give up their best room to him. But this he would not hear of. Pat Rooney only rented three rooms and a small kitchen on the second floor; one was a sitting-room, the two others bedrooms. In one of the latter, Pat, his wife, and the youngest child slept; in the other the two eldest children. In the sitting and dining-room was an old sofa. On this Noel elected to sleep, and would hear of no other arrangement.

He would rather have slept in the street than have disturbed their arrangements.

Pat had only been at work four days, so that he could not expect any money till Saturday night. Consequently the Rooneys were full of apologies for not offering him anything better for supper than bread and cheese and porter. The former had been borrowed from the neighbours, and the beer had been supplied on credit by the public-house people. "Shure, your honour, it's the best we can do till the good time comes; it's bad wid all of us now: if there was cold mate in any house in the court, it should be yours."

Noel drew his little stock of silver from his pocket, and handed it to Pat, saying,

"This is all I have in the world; when I shall get any more I cannot say with certainty, though I hope it will not be long before I obtain employment; take this money, my friend, and do what you like with it for our common benefit."

This created a new furore in Noel's favour. The supper that evening was by mutual consent improved for the better. Noel was neutral in the matter; he said nothing. Pat was strongly in favour of trotters; but Rosha, being backed up by the children, voted for wilks or mussels. Finding himself unsupported, Pat was about to give way and submit to the delicacy proposed by his wife, when Noel, not fancying either one or the other, suggested some cold ham and beef, to be purchased at the cookshop.

This at first was regarded as the height of extravagance; but as the evening celebrated an event, and ought to be one of festivity, trotters and wilks faded away into the dim and misty obscurity of the imagination, and Pat lighted his pipe, while Rosha went to market.

The next day Noel went out for a walk. He could give no particular reason for doing so; but he held that no good was to be done by staying at home; Fortune seldom came to those who did not look for her and give her an invitation.

He strayed into an aristocratic part of the town, and was walking round the enclosure of a large square, when he heard the sound of horses' hoofs, and a shrill cry of " Save her !—save her ! Save my daughter !" broke upon his ears.

Looking up, he saw a horse, black as jet, passionately excited with the bit between its teeth, tearing along at a great pace; on its back was a girl, young, beautiful, probably accomplished, unquestionably very much alarmed. She was clinging to the creature's mane, and had lost her seat at the same time that she lost all control over the animal.

To stop a horse galloping at full speed is not only a courageous but a dangerous task; yet surely it was only manly of Noel to dash forward, utterly regardless of risk, and after two unsuccessful attempts to grasp the bridle of the infuriated and maddened steed.

What matter that he was dragged some distance, to the imminent danger of life and limb? what matter that the insensate brute nearly crushed him beneath his iron-shod feet? Did not the man who had exclaimed in piteous accents, " Save her ! save her !—save my daughter !" and who was presumably her father, ride up in haste, and stop the horse, ere he could do Noel a mischief ?

Noel rose, covered with blood and dust; for he had

not escaped scot-free, and was just in time to receive in
his open arms the falling body of the young lady, who,
unable to keep her senses any longer, succumbed to the
terror of the moment.

When the father discovered that his daughter was
unhurt, his gratitude was immense.

It seemed to be Noel's fate that week to place people
under obligations to him.

A passing fly was hailed; and the lady's inanimate
body placed within it.

The groom had secured the horses; and the girl's
father, before driving away in the fly, exclaimed,

"I do not know who you are, sir; but you have
rendered me a signal service, and I shall be most
charmed to make your acquaintance. You have unquestionably saved my dear daughter's life, which is
equivalent to having saved mine—for I should not long
have survived her. Since her mother's death she has
been my only treasure. Here is my card. Pray call
upon me at your earliest convenience. Excuse my
hurry, for Alma must be at once attended to."

Noel took the card, and the gentleman directed the
flyman to drive to 81 Brunswick-square.

While Noel was watching the retreating fly, and
wondering at the strange adventure which had befallen
him, the groom, leading the two horses, came up and
said, with a respectful salutation,

"Just in time, sir."

Noel turned round; and then the groom perceived
that he was shabbily dressed, and looked more like an
adventurer upon whom fortune smiles not, than a gentleman. The groom thought he had made a mistake.
Was he not addressing an equal, or perhaps an inferior?

Finding that Noel did not answer him, he changed his manner, and said,

" Lucky thing for you, mister—you'll get something handsome."

Without noticing him, Noel strode away ; and looking at the card, saw that he had saved the life of the daughter of Levison Maitland, Esq., of Maitland, whoever that might be. That her name was Alma he already knew, for her father had called her so. His innate gentlemanly feeling told him that it would be better for him to call in the course of the next day.

When he returned to Eden-gardens he heard the sound of grief proceeding from Pat Rooney's house. Some one was weeping, and making deep lamentation.

Fearful lest some accident had happened to Pat, who was a bricklayer by trade, he hastened on, and, addressing an Irishwoman, inquired what was the matter.

" Whist !" she said, holding her finger to her lips and looking at him with aversion. " Shure, an' it was the bad day when you crassed the threshold—it's no luck at all at all they've had since."

" But will you explain ?" cried Noel, much puzzled.

The woman was about to reply, when Patrick himself entered the court, singing blithely, " Lero, lero, lillibullero."

Suddenly he stopped.

What was all that weeping and wailing occasioned by ? Did it not proceed from his own house ? Was it not his wife Rosha's voice ?

A man kindly disposed, but a sad blunderer, separated himself from the crowd, and, going up to Rooney, exclaimed, as he laid his hand kindly on his shoulder,

" Pat !"

"Well; what is the matter beyant?"

"I want a word with you."

"With me?" he replied, adding as a thought struck him, "his honour, God bless him—is he hurted?"

"No; it isn't that. It's one of your little ones in the water."

"Mine! Drowned!" exclaimed the Irishman, in a broken-hearted voice. "O Lord! The praste tould me something would happen bekase of our sins."

The shock made him reel like a drunken man.

He half-staggered to his own doorstep, and sat down, covering his face with his hands, through the half-closed fingers of which the tears trickled, and fell on the flags in big burning drops, like heat-spots before thunder.

It appeared that the child had gone to the sea-side, and was playing with some companions, when he lost his balance and fell into the water, from which he was never extricated alive.

Rosha had been summoned to the place where the accident took place; and her grief was pitiful to witness. When the drags brought up the boy's cap she said,

"That's me darlint's cap. O, save me child!"

All their efforts were vain.

The child was brought to the shore a corpse.

Noel endeavoured, to the best of his ability, to comfort the afflicted family; but she wept for her child, and would not be comforted.

Some of the superstitious Irish people living in the court attributed the calamity to Noel's presence beneath the roof of Pat Rooney; but Pat was too large-minded to join in this foolish cry.

Noel had heard it said that the poor do not love their children. He had his own opinion about the matter after what he saw that evening in Eden-gardens. Grief in its purest form was there and then exhibited; and tears were wrung from the eyes of the most callous bystander.

CHAPTER VIII.

A CHANGE OF FORTUNE.

WHEN the morning dawned, cold, foggy, and autumnal, Noel wended his way to Brunswick-square, where lived his new friends the Maitlands. He did not care about fee or reward; but the face of the pretty girl whose life he had saved haunted him, and he longed to behold her once more.

It may not be inappropriate to say a word or two about the family. The Maitlands of Maitland, as they loved to hear themselves called, were a very ancient family. They scorned the idea of coming over with the Conqueror, though they admitted that Norman blood flowed in their veins. They talked dimly, not to say wildly, about Hengist and Horsa, and now and then of Boadicea; leaving people to draw their own conclusions from these mysterious and cloudy hints.

In the days of bad roads and indifferent coaches, they never dreamt of going to Brighton in the season; but the railway effected a revolution in their habits, and then they never missed the fashionable period at Brighton.

In their own county they were thought a great deal of, but in Brighton or London they were, comparatively

speaking, lost amidst a shoal of fish as big as themselves. Mr. Maitland had once sat in Parliament, but
his political career was a failure. His constituents were
not satisfied with their representative, and when the
inevitable general election came they, with all the una-
nimity in the world, turned him out, and gave the seat
to another if not a worthier man. Having been accustomed to spend the winter in the country and Brighton,
and the summer in town, Mr. Maitland could not divest
himself of the habit, though he was strongly tempted
on the death of his wife and the loss of his borough,
which, oddly enough, happened almost simultaneously,
to retire into the country and there vegetate till the end
of his days. He had, however, one great inducement to
go into society, and this was the fact of his having a
daughter to marry. Alma was not only a paragon of
loveliness, but one of the sweetest-tempered girls in a
happy land, where amiable and lovely girls are as plenti-
ful as blackberries. No wonder that the proud father
loved his daughter. She did all she could to endear
herself to him, and never gave him in all her life one
moment's uneasiness. Loving his darling Alma as
father has rarely loved before, it is not in any way remarkable that Mr. Maitland should feel an exaggerated
sense of obligation towards Noel.

When our hero arrived, about half-past eleven
o'clock, at the house in Brunswick-square, he was
ushered into a splendidly-furnished drawing-room, with
much taste and ceremony, by a footman in gorgeous
livery and unsullied plush. Here he was shortly afterwards joined by Mr. Maitland, who recognised him in
a moment, and wrung him heartily by the hand, saying,
" I have been anxiously looking for you, my dear sir.

I wish to thank you for the inestimable service you rendered me yesterday. I assure you I am everlastingly yours to command.

"I trust Miss Maitland, sir, has experienced no ill effects from the fright she must have endured yesterday?" said Noel.

"None at all, I am happy to say. She is in excellent health, and not a bit the worse. Indeed, she talks of going out riding again, which, I am afraid, is a little venturous : but I will take care she has a quieter hack. Will you come and see her, or stay? She is finishing some letters. By the time you and I have had some conversation she will have ended her task, and I will let her know that her preserver is waiting to see her. Did she but guess you were here, she would fly to express her gratitude."

Noel had brushed his coat as well as he could, and had had the holes in it patched up by an unprofessional hand ; but the garment was sadly threadbare, and scarcely the sort of coat in which a gentleman — for such he felt himself to be—would present himself to the presence of a lady.

"Take a chair, my dear sir," continued Mr. Maitland, "and let me know all about you. Do not think me impertinent, or curiously intrusive. I want to be of service to you."

Noel told the old gentleman everything, from his father's death to Sir Charles Evander's coldness, and his present unhappy position, concealing nothing.

"All that shall cease," said Mr. Maitland, alluding to his distress. "If you want employment, I can obtain it for you. You are experienced in book-keeping, I presume?"

"I think I should soon understand the routine business of a merchant's counting-house."

"Very well. What do you say, then, to three hundred a-year for your services from nine till six?" said Mr. Maitland, with an amiable smile.

"What do I say?" cried Noel, almost wild with sudden joy. "I say, my dear sir, that I can scarcely bring myself to believe in such good fortune."

"Nevertheless it shall be a fact. You will find me essentially practical. I never thank people with empty words; I give them some tangible proof of my gratitude and esteem."

Noel murmured his thanks in an incoherent manner; and Mr. Maitland left him to recover himself while he went to fetch his daughter.

What a wonderful change in four-and-twenty hours had taken place in Noel's fortunes! His chivalrous and unselfish conduct had been rewarded in a manner little expected by him; for when he saved Alma Maitland's life, by stopping a runaway horse at the risk of broken limbs and a dire catastrophe, he never dreamed of fee or reward; yet when a means of getting his own living was offered him, he could not refuse it.

Had Mr. Maitland placed a purse of twenty or thirty guineas in his hand, he would have blushed to take it — his pride would have forbidden him to do so, and he would have returned the gold to the liberal but impolitic donor.

Alma entered the room—her face suffused with blushes, and her eyes beaming grateful glances at her preserver.

Noel was instantly struck with her beauty.

She wore a light flowered muslin, cinctured at the

waist by a broad sash of mauve ribbon. Her golden
hair was plaitèd, and fastened behind with a comb;
while a pretty curl hung gracefully over each shoulder.

She extended the whitest and smallest hand, having
the prettiest pink almond-shaped nails that it was ever
woman's fortunate lot to have. Noel lost no time in
grasping it, though he did so rather timidly.

In a clear voice, which ran through the room like
the tinkling of a silver bell, Alma said,

"It gives me much pleasure, Mr. Evander, to be
able to thank you in person for so gallantly saving my
life yesterday. Believe me when I say that I shall never
forget it—never, never!"

"Indeed you lay too much stress upon a trifling act
that any one would have been glad to be the author of,"
replied Noel.

"O, no! Pardon my contradicting you. Had it
not been for you, I might now be lying crushed and
mangled upon my bed, with broken limbs and disfigured
features."

"Pray do not conjure up such horrors, Miss Maitland," Noel exclaimed, with a deprecatory gesture.

Some further conversation took place, and then Alma
retired, expressing a hope that she might have the pleasure of seeing Noel again shortly. Her father satisfied
her upon that point, and she tripped away gaily like a
sunbeam.

When they were alone again, Mr. Maitland placed
a cheque for twenty pounds in Noel's hand. The young
man made a gesture indicative of dissent, and would
have returned the draft had not the giver said, "Do not
be hasty; I want you to accept this as a loan. When
you have been a short time at work, you can repay me.

You must not be too delicate, for you have, no doubt, many demands upon your purse."

On the understanding that the money was given him as a loan, Noel took it with many thanks. Mr. Maitland said he would that very day go into the office of his friends, Messrs. Cunliffe, Harding, and Strevor, and make arrangements for Noel to begin his career as their clerk as early as possible.

"You see, my dear young friend, that I take an interest in you," exclaimed Mr. Maitland, with a fatherly smile.

"You are very good to say so, sir," replied Noel, highly gratified at so complimentary a speech.

"You saved the life of my daughter at the risk of your own, and you have thereby established your claim to my gratitude; for since my poor wife's death, I have centred all my love and affection on Alma. She is the darling and the pet of my age; and I am not exaggerating when I say that had anything happened to her—had she been killed, in fact—I should never have held up my head again."

"I assure you, sir, that I had no expectation of reward. I was not actuated by mercenary motives in what I did. I wished to do to another as I hoped to be done by in a similar position."

"I am fully aware of that; but it is not my wish that your disinterestedness should go unrewarded. You will find yourself very much at home at Messrs. Cunliffe, Harding, and Strevor's. They will treat you with every kindness and consideration, for they are under obligations to me, and my recommendation is the very best you could bring them. All I say to you is—do your duty. Endeavour to give satisfaction, and your connection with the firm may, in a few years' time, turn out more advantageously than you have any idea of. I am not a prophet, and make no prediction, but this I will say—clerks very frequently become partners."

"I shall be perfectly content, sir, if I can make sure of the handsome income you have been good enough to promise me," said Noel.

"That is certain; make your mind perfectly easy on that score," returned Mr. Maitland. "I hope we shall often have the pleasure of seeing you. Make yourself *ami de la maison,* for you will always be a welcome guest."

Noel was so overpowered with pleasurable emotions that he was unable to reply to Mr. Maitland, who shook him cordially by the hand, and showed him the way out, opening the front door with his own hands.

It was with a bounding heart that Noel left Mr. Maitland's house in Brunswick-square. He was full of gratitude to the Dispenser of all good things. Adversity had chastened him, and he was not unduly elated by prosperity. A short time before he was a homeless wanderer; now he was a man in a position, surrounded by influential friends, and, what was more, he had twenty pounds in his pocket.

Having changed his cheque at the bank, he took a respectable lodging, leaving the Rooneys without much regret, promising to keep up his acquaintance with them. He also bought himself such clothing as a man in his position in life stood in need of, and he felt he could once more engage in the battle of life without a sinking heart.

The Rooneys were broken-hearted at the idea of Noel leaving them. During the short time he had resided with them in that intra-mural paradise, Eden-gardens, he had contrived to endear himself to one and all; and Rosha shed many tears when she heard that her kind-hearted guest was going away.

Noel had enjoyed an opportunity of studying the Irish character, and he formed a favourable opinion of the sons of Erin.

A warmer-hearted creature than Patrick Rooney he had never met with; and though always poor, and squalid, and in rags, he was ever generous and honest.

"And is it going you are?" said Patrick.

"I must go, my friend," replied Noel. "A change has taken place in my position and prospects. But go I must, although I leave you with every feeling of regret."

"The good God will bless you, Misther Noel," replied the Irishman; "for shure ye've been the darlint of all our hearts since ye've been among us."

"I am glad to hear that: for I would always rather make friends than enemies."

"If we were in ould Ireland," said Patrick Rooney, "we'd give you a wake to-night. I wish'd I were going wid you, Misther Noel—but it's all for the best, and we shall see you again. It was you who saved the bed from being sould from undher me; and Patrick Rooney's not the boy to forget it. May the Virgin smile upon you!"

At this moment Rosha, holding a handkerchief to her eyes, came into the room, and shaking Noel by the hand, said,

"It's a hard thing to lose a friend, sir, for you've been a good friend to us."

"And so have you to me, Mrs. Rooney," said Noel. "You forget that I am under obligations to you and your husband."

"Ay, but that's nothing. What have you had with us but a bite and a sup and a bit of a bed? Och! to talk of it is more than it's worth. Pat will do any thing for you, sir. It was only last night that Shaun O'Sullivan, in the court here, was a saying somethink about you, when up came Pat, and says he,

'You dhirty omathawn, what's that ye're saying? You'd best keep your tongue betwane your teeth, or you'll have an attack of your ould complaint, the falling sickness.'

"But Shaun had the dhrop, do you see, sir, and he wouldn't be still, and he went on to say somethink about you; so Pat, giving a whoop and a jump in the air, gave him the Donnybrook touch, and down he went like a hundred o' bricks. And he'd do that same to any of 'em, if he got a week for it, or a month on bread-and-water, and having no mate, nor even a dhrop of the cratur."

At last Noel shook off his kind friends, offered them some money, which they steadfastly refused to take, and wishing them every sort of luck and prosperity, went away to his new domicile.

CHAPTER IX.

"LA BEATA."

MESSRS. CUNLIFFE, HARDING, and STREVOR were under many obligations to Mr. Maitland, the nature of which it is unnecessary to describe and dilate upon here. Let it suffice to state, that they at once consented to take

G

Noel into their employment, and to give him the somewhat munificent sum, for a young beginner, of one
hundred and fifty pounds per annum.

Noel entered upon his work within a week, and gave
entire satisfaction to his employers, who found him a
sharp, shrewd man of business, a good accountant, and
strictly punctual in every thing he undertook. Sometimes he would stay at the office as late as ten o'clock at
night without asking to be paid for overtime, and was,
in fact, the willing horse of the office. His employers
did not work him to death, however ; they were sensible
enough to know when they had a good servant. They
were wine-merchants in a large way of business, and
had an establishment in Brighton as well as in London,
allowing Noel to work in the Brighton counting-house, as
he was near the Maitlands, and seemed to prefer the
sea-side to town.

One day Mr. Cunliffe asked him if he had any money,
or if he could obtain any: for if so, he would advise him
to go and purchase a certain kind of merchandise in
which he was assured there would be a rise within a
week.

Noel took the hint, and borrowed fifty pounds from
Mr. Maitland, with which he speculated so judiciously
on Mr. Cunliffe's advice, that he trebled it. This was
a fortunate event for him. He repaid Mr. Maitland
the money he had borrowed, and opened a banking account with what remained; thus acquiring a position,
and feeling that whatever betided, he would not be destitute and penniless as he had been twice before.

It is astonishing, too, how this windfall raised him in
his own estimation. He went about his work with more
interest, and was altogether an altered man.

He was a frequent guest at Mr. Maitland's, and Alma ever welcomed him with a hearty smile and an outstretched hand. He derived more pleasure from his visits to Brunswick-square than from anything else. All at once it struck him, as he was diving into his own heart, in obedience to that invaluable precept " Know thyself," that he was steering towards a terrible Charybdis.

He at first regarded Alma Maitland as a lovely being, rather more seraphic than terrestrial; then he looked upon her as a charming young lady, accomplished and winning, whom it was his proudest boast to call his friend; thirdly, it seemed to him that he was beginning to love this seraphic being.

What presumption! How could he —poor, unknown, a clerk, hope to marry so peerless a creature as Alma Maitland? Unutterable presumption! It was folly of the highest kind; a Titan trying to scale the sides of Olympus was not more foolish, more egregiously in the wrong.

And it was more than presumptuous; it was ungrateful. For Mr. Maitland, with the loquacious fondness of a doting father, would often talk of his Alma making a " good match by and by."

A good match? Was Noel Evander a good match? Far from it. Perhaps if Alma saw that he loved her, she would, as love begets love, come in time to regard him with anything but indifference. If Noel stole Alma's heart away, he would be dealing Mr. Maitland the severest blow he had it in his power to deliver; for although the old gentleman was the quintessence of kindness, he was very proud, and would have died sooner than his daughter should have mated with one below her in the social scale—and so much below her too, as was Noel.

So Noel, pondering all these things in his fond, foolish heart, kept away as much as possible from the house in Brunswick-square, pretending that business had charms which were too potent to be withstood. He deluded himself with the idea, and so did he delude others ; but if he could have read himself and his inclinations aright, he would have cast books and ledgers from him, and have become a love-sick nonentity.

There was one person in the house in the square who has not yet been introduced to the reader. This was a lady, the family name of whose house was La Beata. Her christian name was Inessa. Grand old blood had she in her veins; but her family had met with reverses, and at four-and-twenty Inessa La Beata found herself an inmate of Mr. Maitland's mansion, the friend, companion, and governess of Alma. There was not so much intimacy between the girls as is usual in such cases; Alma rather feared Inessa, she was so lynx-like and so tigerish at times. And O what glorious passions she would sometimes put herself in ! It was like a monsoon sweeping over the bosom of a perturbed and angry sea.

She blamed her fiery southern blood for all this; and when she was calm and still, serene as the lake of Como when moonlit, she was so fascinating, so incomparably charming, that it was a delight and a pleasure to be in her society.

Inessa never thoroughly revealed herself to any one —not even to Alma. She was always a blushing rose-bud, some day to unfold its leaves, but defying any amount of good-tempered genial sunshine to force her to open her petals.

Noel admired—almost reverenced her; but he did not love her. Fragile, gentle, pretty Alma was made to be loved; but Inessa La Beata was too stern, too queen-like, too majestic to be aught but worshipped at a distance.

Yet there was a charm — a strange, inexplicable charm, in her society. Noel often found himself sitting with La Beata, while Alma was neglected.

One Saturday evening Noel was at Brunswick-square. Mr. Maitland had driven out, and he had called at Cunliffe and Harding's for Noel, whom he insisted should come back to dine with him.

Noel found it impossible to refuse compliance with this request.

Dinner being over, Mr. Maitland was in an arm-chair enjoying a "gentle doze." Alma was playing herself into a dreamy state at the piano, over some sweet sonata of Beethoven's; she was utterly uncon-scious of any one's presence; the music soothed and enthralled her, because she understood it, and inter-preted it so exquisitely with the aid of the admirable instrument upon which she was playing.

Somehow or other, Noel and Inessa were together. They sat upon a sociable at the end of the room. Against the wall a great mass of flowers was artistically arranged, emitting a most delicious perfume. Inessa spoke to Noel.

" Do you like Beethoven's music?" she asked.

" I like it. It soothes me; but I am not musical, and cannot understand it. If you can tell what I mean, I will say, that it is like some one speaking to me in a foreign language—your own, for instance; the sweet tones please my ear, but I attach no meaning to them."

" Perhaps you like the executant better than you do the music;" said La Beata, fixing her large, lustrous, Juno-like eyes upon him—full upon him, till he lowered his before the searching gaze.

" I—like—the—executant!" repeated Noel, slowly, and emphasising the word *like*. " What do you mean?"

" Simply this.   I am in the full possession of my seven senses.   I can see, hear, and understand; and I have come to a conclusion."

" Which is——"

" That you love Alma Maitland."

Noel shook his head sadly.   For a moment he was lost in thought.   Then he looked up, and said,

" I believe you are my friend.   If so, permit me to undeceive you on one point.   However much I may respect and esteem Miss Maitland, I can never love her."

" Why?" said Inessa, elevating her eyebrows at the same time that she expressively shrugged her shoulders.

" I will tell you.   I can never love her, because I will not permit myself to do so."

" That very remark shows me that you already love her," said La Beata, with a mocking laugh.   " If you do regard her with affection, why not marry her?"

" Marry her!" cried Noel, with a startled look. " No, no!   Sooner would I cut my right hand off."

" You are very foolish," replied Inessa La Beata. " I can tell you that Alma does not dislike you.   If you can obtain a pretty wife and a good connection at the same time, is it not worth the while of a man in your position to do so?"

"In my position?" said Noel, a little hurt. "If I am nothing more, I hope I am an honest man."

"And that, your poet says, is the 'noblest work of God.'"

"Whatever may be my fate," said Noel, sententiously, "and it is not for me to presume to raise the veil of the future, I will never subject myself to the reproach of having been ungrateful to the man who lent me a helping hand when I most needed it."

"But you forget that you saved his daughter's life."

"That does not enter into my consideration."

"It should do so. It was what you call tit for tat. *You* saved Alma—*he* put you in the way of getting your own living."

"It is an ungrateful dog that bites the hand that feeds it," said Noel.

"You are becoming prosy and proverbial. You do not see the force of my argument, and you are clearly not a man of the world. If you love Alma Maitland——"

"Excuse me, I never said so."

"I am aware of that—I advanced the *fact;* but if you do, and she is not unfavourable to your suit, why turn away from your Eldorado?"

"Simply because I am an honest man, Mademoiselle La Beata, and not an ungrateful scoundrel," replied Noel, with dignity.

Inessa contemplated the young man with an expression of pity. It seemed inconceivable to her that any one should neglect a chance of making his fortune, when the blind and fickle goddess smiled upon him.

"In what would your ingratitude consist?" she said. "Frankly, I am at a loss to understand you."

"I will tell you," responded Noel, promptly. "Mr. Maitland has taken me by the hand, and given me his countenance; but he never for a moment suspects that I contemplate robbing him of his daughter. From what I know of Mr. Maitland, I am persuaded that he is ambitious, and wishes his child to marry some one who would confer lustre upon the family. There are many men of title, wealth, and position, who would be proud to marry so peerless and accomplished a lady as Miss Maitland. She is the perfection of feminine beauty—a paragon of loveliness."

Inessa smiled.

"For my part," she exclaimed, with a shrug of the shoulders, "I cannot see what there is to admire in doll-like beauty. If I were a man, I should despise flaxen hair like floss silk, and a shrinking, timid, child-like woman, who wears a saintly expression upon her meaningless face, has no will of her own, and can never say you nay."

"One of my peculiarities is, that I admire just the sort of delicate, fragile creature you have been describing," replied Noel.

"In that case you have found your ideal in Miss Maitland," replied Inessa La Beata, with a smile.

Noel blushed.

"You are young, Mr. Evander," resumed Inessa. "If you had worn off the rust of youth, and acquired the polish of travel—(pray don't think me rude or impertinent)—you would scarcely entertain such an exaggerated opinion of doll-like beauty as you do at present. In my country women are not always tame and quiet, like mill-ponds. They at times resemble the ocean when asleep; but they as often resemble it when en-

raged and lashed into tempestuous fury by the force of
the winds. In Italy we have the stiletto; and more—
we know how to use it."

"That, surely, is not a recommendation."

"I did not advance it as such. I simply state a
fact."

"A passionate woman is very often a shrew," said
Noel.

"No; pardon me. A passionate woman is never
shrewish. She rises beyond herself in all the mighty
grandeur of a sudden passion, and speedily exhausts herself by her efforts; then she is placid and docile."

"Would she not be preferable without the excitement?"

"That is a matter of taste. If I were going to buy
a horse, I should prefer an animal that requires the
curb, and will not bear the touch of a whip."

"There is less trouble, though, with one that will
run in a snaffle," remarked Noel.

"It is less elegant, and not so much admired."

"Let us abandon the equine digression," remarked
Noel. "If I were to marry, I should not like my wife
to be admired by everybody. I should be jealous of the
least attention being paid her. In fact, I should keep
her shut up, and have her society all to myself."

"No woman in the world would tolerate that," cried
Inessa La Beata, with a sparkling laugh. "We are not
birds, to be caged, Mr. Evander. You will find that
out some day, when you know us better. You must
forgive me for laughing; but really the ideas that some
young men have about women are intensely provocative
of mirth. You would have a wife who, if subjected to
close analysis, is little better than a goose; depend upon

it though, however amiable a woman may seem before marriage, she will develope afterwards, and show you that apple-eating mother Eve handed down some frailties to her sex. Now, answer me truly, at present you cannot discover a single imperfection in Miss Maitland?"

"You are quite right. I cannot."

"You think her absolutely angelic?"

"I do."

"And I, who know her well, could point out a dozen imperfections."

"Perhaps it would be a congenial task to do so," said Noel, a little nettled.

"Why?" asked Inessa La Beata, biting her lips.

"O, I don't know," he answered, carelessly. "Perhaps I spoke foolishly."

"Do not be in doubt about it. Admit it at once. Pray do not fancy yourself an Adonis, and a lady-killer, Mr. Evander, simply because I happened to tell you that I fancied Miss Maitland had a fondness for you. It does not follow that every lady is to tread in the same girlish footsteps. If you were a distinguished man—an author, artist, millionaire, or what not, I could understand your being a little confident and exacting; but true merit is always modest and unassuming. Are you not aware of that fact?"

Noel cast down his eyes and looked abashed.

"You are young," continued Inessa La Beata. "I had occasion to make the same remark once before this evening; so you see I am losing my originality. One must always be lenient with the young. To break flies upon the wheel may be an amusing occupation, but with me it is not a congenial one. I simply told you as a friend that you might pay your addresses in a certain quarter without fearing a repulse."

"And I answer you candidly, Miss Beata, that I will do nothing of the sort," replied Noel, resolutely.

"Very well. All I can say is, so much the worse for you."

"You are counselling that which I can never stoop to."

"Pardon me, I am counselling nothing. I was performing an act of friendship, and I begin to regret that I undertook so thankless an office, and interested myself in so ungrateful and unappreciative a person as yourself."

She spoke somewhat acrimoniously, which Noel did not notice.

"Many thanks for your kindness, Miss Beata," he said. "But I am sufficiently a man of honour to refuse to tempt Miss Maitland to break her father's heart. He is, I am proud to say, my friend and patron; and until I receive encouragement from him I am dumb, even if my silence should cause me more pain and anguish than I can find words to express."

Inessa was about to return to the charge, when a servant announced some visitors—"Mr. Gore Markby and Sir Charles Evander."

"Ah!" exclaimed Mr. Maitland, waking up, "my very good friend Gore Markby and Sir Charles. Show them up. Dear me. I promised to meet them at the Pavilion, and the appointment entirely escaped my memory. How very provoking, to be sure! Never mind, let them come up; I must apologise."

Noel's heart beat quickly when he heard that Sir Charles Evander was coming into the room. He did not know then that he was the usurper of his property, but he knew that he had treated him very unkindly, and he wondered how he would meet him.

To his surprise Evander took no notice of him, though he started as their eyes met, and began to talk to Alma, who disliked him greatly. She answered in monosyllables, and turned away her head when he spoke to her, which much delighted Noel.

The fact was, Sir Charles had taken a fancy to Alma, but finding he received no encouragement he went over to Mr. Maitland and talked to him, while Mr. Markby, the representative of an old county family, led Alma to the piano, and turned over the leaves of the music for her.

Noel was unable to prevent casting an anxious glance occasionally in Sir Charles Evander's direction. "Coming events cast their shadows before." He could not help thinking, or, let me say, feeling instinctively, that Sir Charles was endeavouring to do him some harm with his kind friend and patron.

Inessa La Beata remarked her companion's uneasiness, and did not fail to ask him the cause. Inessa was just the sort of woman calculated to advise and lead a young man. There was something commanding in her superb, queen-like beauty, and her manner was such as to invite confidence. Noel always talked to La Beata as he would to an elder sister.

"Come, tell me," she said, "you and your namesake, Sir Charles, have met before. Is it not so?"

"We have," replied Noel, a little reluctantly.

"I thought so. Am I not a good diviner? You must tell me all about it; for I confess to a little curiosity."

"I would rather not tell you. I have only mentioned that passage in my life to Mr. Maitland."

"Indeed! Is it one of which you are ashamed?"

"Heaven forbid that I should be ashamed of anything I ever did in my life!" cried Noel, rather loudly. "No, I was not ashamed; I was merely mortified and disappointed. This I will tell you; Sir Charles is my cousin, and has not treated me well."

"Really! And yet you pretend to be strangers to one another. So you will not enlighten my ignorance?"

"Another time, if you will kindly allow me."

"O, certainly; I will not press you for your confidence. If I have it at all, it shall be spontaneous," said Inessa, looking slightly annoyed.

"How my ears burn!" said Noel.

"Some one is talking about you; probably Sir Charles."

"At that I should not wonder," Noel answered, getting red in the face, and altogether uncomfortable.

La Beata's conjecture that Sir Charles Evander was talking about Noel was not incorrect. After conversing upon indifferent subjects for some time, he said, in a low but significant tone of voice, "I rather fancy I have seen that young man before." He pointed to Noel as he spoke.

"Yes; he has told me that you are his cousin. He is a clerk in Cunliffe and Harding's. I got him in."

"Pray, may I ask what induced you to interest yourself in such a fellow?"

"Such a fellow! My dear Sir Charles, what do you mean?" said Mr. Maitland, with surprise depicted upon his eloquent countenance.

"I have heard bad accounts of him, and for that

reason I would not interest myself on his account,"
said Evander. " I gave him a slight gratuity and dismissed him, when he called upon me begging and trying to extort money; and I thought no more about the
matter until just now, when I saw this precious Mr.
Noel Evander in your house, when it appeared to me
to be my duty to put you on your guard."

" Exactly; thank you," said Mr. Maitland, drily.
" I can easily account for his presence here. He was
enabled, under Providence, one day to save my daughter
Alma's life. Her horse had run away with her, and in
all human probability she would have been killed had it
not been for his active intervention. As a matter of
course, I felt deeply grateful, and so did Alma. We
have shown him every kindness since then, and I feel
impelled by a sense of justice to state that we have
found him uniformly gentlemanly and straightforward.
It was only the other day that Cunliffe himself told
me he would trust Noel with thousands; he had not for
some time met with a man in whom he had such confidence."

" Well, well; you speak as you find," said Sir
Charles Evander, " and you are quite right to do so.
I only speak from my own experience; and knowing
Cunliffe and Harding so well, I shall consider it only
right and proper to make the same statement to them
as I have to you. It would be agreeable to them,
certainly, to wake up some morning and find the
safe broken open, the money and securities gone, and
some one else, who shall be nameless, gone along with
them."

" You are harsh, Sir Charles. I cannot say that my
opinions coincide with yours. I confess to a liking for

Noel. I have always found him honest. What more do I want?"

"That is true enough; the time may come though when you will see things through a different medium. But come, we are neglecting the music."

When the music was over Sir Charles noticed that Mr. Maitland was very silent. Suddenly the latter exclaimed, "You can have no objection to my mentioning to Noel, in your presence, what you have just alleged against him. A highly respectable man like yourself need fear nothing from—"

"Certainly not," replied Sir Charles, with a scornful laugh; "my position is too well known and defined for any trumped-up absurdity to do me any harm. By all means call the fellow here, and say what you like to him. He cannot deny what I have stated, though he may perhaps feel called upon to favour us with some explanation of his extraordinary conduct."

"He has a name; why talk of him in that contemptuous manner? Why say 'that fellow,' when it would be so much more courteous to speak of him by his name?"

"I beg your pardon, I'm sure," replied Sir Charles Evander, loftily; "for the moment I forgot that he was your protégé."

"He saved my daughter's life," answered Mr. Maitland. "Need I say more than that?"

He beckoned with his hand to Noel, who, making an apology to Inessa La Beata, walked across the room promptly. Sir Charles stared insolently at him, with a view of discomposing his serenity; but he failed miserably in the effort. Mr. Maitland exclaimed,

"Do you know this gentleman?"

"I have seen him."

"Under what circumstances?"

"As he has most probably given you the history of our brief acquaintance, it is almost superfluous for me to repeat it."

"Let me ask you to recapitulate, for my own satisfaction?"

"No, sir, I will not; I am not on my trial. I simply came to Sir Charles Evander to ask for a little relief under extraordinary circumstances; he refused it, and I have not seen him since."

"Then you had no intention of extorting money, as he says?" exclaimed Mr. Maitland.

He was sorry for saying it afterwards; the pained expression of Noel's face was so piteous, that it would have touched a heart of stone. Noel saw that some of the double-distilled poison of Sir Charles had sunk into his patron's mind, or at all events left its taint behind it. He did not say anything in his vindication; he did not attempt to exculpate himself; he did not exclaim indignantly against the accusation; he simply said, "Good-bye, Mr. Maitland," in so sad a tone of voice, that a heavy sadness fell upon the gentleman as he listened to its plaintive cadence.

"Good-bye! Why, what—where are you going?"

He received no answer; Noel had turned proudly away. To Inessa La Beata and Alma he bowed; he could not trust himself to speak to either of them. Had he spoken to Alma, he would have broken down completely, and have shed a flood of tears, which would have shamed his manhood. Inessa opened her big eyes wider than usual. There was a mystery in all that was taking place that she would have given much to solve.

Alma went on playing, utterly unconscious of anything unpleasant having happened.

In a moment Noel was in the hall. He waited for no servant to help him on with his hat and coat; he threw one over his arm, put the other on his head, and sallied forth into the night, shaking off the dust from his feet ere he went.

Dark clouds rolled overhead, but they were not blacker than was Noel Evander's desolate heart that night.

CHAPTER X.

A CHANGE OF FORTUNE.

NOEL did not reach his lodgings until some hours after leaving Brunswick-square. His mind was perturbed, and he walked about in a violent manner, as if wishing to utterly exhaust himself, and so subdue the fire that was consuming him.

He had never anticipated that Sir Charles Evander would destroy his little paradise. He had built himself a bower of roses, in which he was happy; but the blight had come, the frost had arrived, and in one hour the work of months was ruined.

Mr. Maitland had thought so much of what Evander had told him, that he had put a question to Noel which the latter thought that he was not justified in putting under any circumstances whatever. The young man's pride had rebelled against suspicion, and he had left the Maitlands, as he thought, for ever. He was young and poor, and he had nothing but his pride to

H

love and cherish. This he nursed unceasingly : although it gave him, at times, a world of trouble, he would not have permitted it to be trampled upon under any consideration.

At length he was driven in by stress of weather. The flood-gates of heaven were opened, and a heavy shower of rain descended, which soon wetted him to the skin. Throwing off his wet clothes, he wrapped himself in the capacious folds of a dressing-gown, and snatched a few hours' uneasy slumber in an arm-chair. Early morning saw him awake again. As he had thought fit to sever his connection with Mr. Maitland, it was only reasonable that he should give Messrs. Cunliffe, Harding, and Strevor notice that he wished to leave their employment ; he had a little money to go on with, and he determined to make a new connection for himself. Surely he could not starve in a land of plenty ; he had met with vicissitudes before, and tided over them all. At first he thought of writing to his employers ; but after a while that idea faded away, and he thought he would call upon them, and give them notice of his intention to leave. He did so.

Mr. Cunliffe was an early man ; but he never reached the office until ten, as it was his invariable custom to go for an hour's ride before breakfast. This was all the exercise he enjoyed, and he found that it did him so much good, that he could not afford to leave it off.

He was literally astounded when he heard Noel's determination to leave. He represented in strong terms the folly of his doing so ; he even held out hopes of a rise in salary, and a more important position in the firm. But Noel was resolute and obstinate. He was determined to find new friends; and he took his leave of Mr. Cunliffe with regret, it is true, but with a feeling of gratified pride. He continued to look out for employment; but he was not successful in his efforts—he knew already that work is not easily obtained. He had some money, as has been already stated, and upon this he lived in an economical manner. But events took place which turned his thoughts into another direction.

One of those terrible convulsions called "panics," which occasionally arrest the operations of commerce, and lay many wealthy houses in a heap of ruins, occurred. Merchants, bankers, stockbrokers and jobbers, discount-houses, contractors—all were concerned in one grand catastrophe.

Barlington and Mowbray, Mr. Maitland's bankers, were much affected by the storm ; and in their distress they came to Mr. Maitland, and asked him if he would place his name on a bill for fifty thousand pounds. Knowing that Barlington and Mowbray were reputed wealthy and reliable, Mr. Maitland did not fail to accede to their request, thinking that he ran no risk thereby, and that he was simply doing an act of kindness to honest men.

Barlington and Mowbray went away with the acceptance, and experienced no difficulty in getting it discounted. The bill was payable one month after date, and the time slipped rapidly away. Still the commercial crisis continued—smash and crash was the order of the day. First some great house would go, and upwards of twenty small houses, as a matter of course, followed in its wake. It was a period of horrid gloom and distress. Men did not sleep at night nor laugh by day; for none knew what disaster might happen next.

The insatiable monster which had been let loose upon mercantile arrangements seemed to be unable to fill his maw.

Mr. Maitland did not make himself at all uneasy about his acceptance. It appeared to him to be a matter of course that Barlington and Mowbray, the great bankers, would take up the bill when it fell due. He was fully aware, that if called upon himself to pay so large a sum of money, he would have to sell every unencumbered acre of land he possessed—the glory of the Maitlands of Maitland would depart from them, and instead of being the proud exclusive aristocrats they were, they would be little better than beggars, dependent upon the precarious alms of the charitable.

This was a side of the picture upon which Mr. Maitland did not look, because he deemed such a casualty of fortune an utter impossibility.

Imagine Mr. Maitland's surprise when, at breakfast one morning, he received a letter asking him if he had made any provision for meeting his acceptance for fifty thousand pounds. The inquiry came upon him like a thunderclap. After the first shock of fright wore off, he tried to laugh.

" O," said he to himself, " it is some mistake on the part of the drawers. Barlington and Mowbray have evidently forgotten, or carelessly overlooked, the bill. I will go into the City at once, give them this letter, and of course the thing will be arranged before the day is out."

Mr. Maitland went up to London at once, and taking a cab at London-bridge, was driven to Lombard-

street, where, at the entrance to the magnificent banking
establishment which he had for years honoured with
his patronage and his custom, he saw a crowd of people.
They were indeed in front of Barlington and Mowbray's place of business. With his heart beating wildly,
he sprang from the cab, and pushing the people on one
side with strong arms, he ascended the steps, and, to
his consternation, found the door of the bank closed.
Upon it was a written notice to the following effect:

" Messrs. Barlington and Mowbray regret to inform
their customers, and the public generally, that owing
to an unexpected pressure, they are unavoidably compelled to suspend payment. Their books have been
placed in the hands of Messrs. Coleman, Turquand,
Youngs, and Co., the well-known accountants, and in a
few days a statement will be made to the creditors."

Mr. Maitland felt stunned, his brain reeled, the
words ran into one another, and the lines of the notice
were hazy and indistinct. Uttering a deep groan, he
fell backwards into the arms of a bystander, who, on
looking upon his pallid face, saw in a moment that he
was insensible.

No wonder the poor gentleman lost his senses; for
he had wit enough to comprehend that, from that day
forth, he and his were comparatively beggars.

The intelligence of Mr. Maitland's reverse of fortune travelled far and wide. Every one heard of it;
and he found few friends who sympathised with him
—or if they did sympathise, it was all they did. The
magnificent estate known as Maitland was brought to
the hammer, and sold to the highest bidder, who hap-

pened to be a City speculator, fancying that the finest
investment of modern times was to buy old estates—to
buy land anywhere and everywhere; for he argued that
as the prosperity of the country increased, and the
number of people with money multiplied, so would the
value of land rise in the market.

Nothing was left Mr. Maitland but a small farm of
about fifty acres, near Brighton. Houses, land, carriage, plate — all went to satisfy the cormorant who
held his acceptance. This man was vindictive; for
Mr. Maitland defended the action which was brought
against him on the bill, and put a plea of "no consideration" on the record. But it did not avail him.
When the alienation of his property was an accomplished and legal fact, Mr. Maitland retired to the
afore-mentioned farm broken-hearted, only kept alive
by his daughter's smiles. And now it was that Alma
really shone, the beauty of her disposition became fully
apparent. She put up with every deprivation and
annoyance, and bore her misfortunes with Christian
humility and resignation.

Assuredly Mr. Maitland would have gone out of his
mind had it not been for Alma.

Inessa La Beata had herself to consider, so it was
scarcely fair to expect her to follow her former friends
into exile. She had her living to get. She did not
wish—in fact, she could not afford—to waste the best
years of her life. Now, in the full springtide of her
beauty, she might get some one to marry her; for beauty
is an equivalent for money any day.

When Noel heard of the reverses which the Maitlands had met with, he was very much grieved. In
their prosperity, he had divorced himself from their

society of his own free will; in their adversity, he resolved to seek them, to make them an offer of his services, without hope of fee or reward—to cast his lot in with theirs, and to show his devotion to them by his disinterestedness.

This was a noble determination, if looked at in the abstract; but perhaps the superlative attraction of Alma's peerless charms had something to do with it. He longed to show Mr. Maitland that, with him, friendship was not merely a name; but, at the same time, he longed ten times as ardently to see Alma, and to watch her demeanour, and note how she bore the calamities that had fallen heavily upon her.

So he started early one morning for Woodbine Farm, the abode of Mr. Maitland and his daughter.

CHAPTER XI.

WOODBINE FARM.

THE farm which remained to Mr. Maitland, as if to remind him of the immense property of which he had been proprietor a short time ago, was situated in a wild and not too-well cultivated part of Sussex. Singularly enough, it was but a few miles distant from the hall at which Sir Charles Evander and his mother sometimes resided, and where Sir Charles retired to shoot over the stubble with a few friends when partridges and pheasants were on the wing.

Distress in the capital had brought distress to the agricultural and manufacturing districts, and the people

in the neighbourhood of Woodbine were not only dis-
contented, but half-starved. Alma had not much to
give away, but what she could spare from her slender
purse she gave to the poor, and her prayers and blessing
went with her alms.

They soon came to know her and love her, these
half-starved people ; but while they loved her, they
hated the Evanders, and above all Sir Charles.

Some folks have a most accomplished knack of
making enemies. The baronet was preëminent in this
respect ; and as he sowed, so did he in after-time reap.

The nearest railway station was six miles from Woodbine ; and as his resources were limited, Noel thought the
best thing he could do would be to inquire the way, and
walk the distance. The road was a pleasant one, chiefly
across country, and he was so well directed, that he stood
but a small chance of missing it.

The sun shone gaily, the birds sang their merriest
carols, the kine lowed in the meadows, the branches of
the trees moved melodiously as a gentle breeze swept
through them ; and Noel walked along with an elastic
step, for his spirits rose within him.

How would the Maitlands receive him ? That was
a question he frequently asked himself. He had been
proud once ; was it not their turn to show that they had
pride in their composition as well as other people ? If
he were driven from the door with an unfeeling rebuff,
that would break his heart, because it would sound the
knell of any hopes he might have entertained respecting
Alma.

The house attached to the farm was one of those
old-fashioned but commodious erections which are to be
met with in country places. It was surrounded by a

large garden studded plentifully with trees, which made
its appearance picturesque. It was just one of those
places to which a philosophic mind, tired of the moil of
great cities, would delight to retire—scarcely the place
for a young girl, to whom the harmless dissipation of life
is a novelty, if not a necessity.

Noel began to steal along like a thief in the night
when he neared the cottage, or farm-house—the latter
being its more dignified name, and maybe its more correct designation. As the garden spread out before him,
the rick-yard was to be seen to the right, and other
buildings to the left; while the quaint old-fashioned
house reared its irregular length in the distance. He
thought that exile in so pretty a place, if shared by
Alma, would not be so very intolerable, after all.

Suddenly he came upon a pretty picture. An immense oak, one of the patriarchs of the forest, overshadowed a large span of grass-plot, in the most shady
part of which was a long rustic seat, made of the gnarled
and twisted boughs of trees artistically put together;
upon this sat Mr. Maitland, his face covered with a
grave shadow, as if mirth had long ago fled that once
jocund countenance. By his side was Alma. She was
a little ruddier than when in London. Her face was
sad, but not nearly so chastened as that of her father.
She was engaged in needlework—it is hard to say of
what description, for the needlework which engages the
attention of ladies in these days is to most men a hidden
mystery.

Noel halted at the back of the tree. He was diffi-
dent, and did not wish to advance all at once. While
hesitating, he heard Alma, who laid down her work on
her lap, with a sigh exclaim : "Papa dear, are you going

to sleep? *Do* talk to me. It gives me the horrors to
see you so miserable."

He started, laughed, and drawing his hand over his
eyes, replied in a tone so altered from his usual quick
spirited style of speaking, that Noel scarcely recognised
the voice.

" What nonsense you talk, Alma! How can I help
being miserable? You ought to talk to me, instead of
petulantly reminding me of my grief."

He looked at her crossly as he spoke.

" Well, don't scold me; I shall cry if you do   I
can't bear being scolded."

" I think over my misfortunes, dear Alma, till I get
irritable," he said gently. " Forgive me."

" O yes, willingly. That is as you ought to talk to
me. You seem to forget that I am not a heroine by any
means, and that I have my own sorrows, just as you
have yours."

" And you are my only consolation. You bear up
nobly, bravely; but I—I am the poltroon."

" No, no, no; you shall not say that."

" But it is true," replied Mr. Maitland. " Yet there
are others in the world. A few months ago, I would not
have believed it possible that all—mark me, all—our
friends would have fled like snow before the morning
sun, as soon as it was known that we had lost our fortune. Why, bless my heart! not even that hot-headed
fellow Noel has thought fit to come near us. Well, well;
they are all alike, and the whole world is not worth a
snap o' the fingers."

Here Noel could contain himself no longer. The
tears had risen to his eyes, and he longed to avow himself. Rushing forward, he caught hold of Mr. Mait-

land's hand—much to that worthy gentleman's terror, for he thought he was about to be garrotted at least—exclaiming,

"You are wrong, my dear sir, in your estimate of human nature. There is one who will not desert you in your altered fortunes. I have come to devote my whole life to you, if you will accept my poor services."

"Why, bless my heart!" cried Mr. Maitland, "can it be Noel? Why, my boy, how did you find us out down here? Sit down by my side. Now, as I am a man, this is kind of you. Yours is the first friendly face I have seen ever since I have been in banishment."

"Have you no word of greeting for *me*, Mr. Evander?" exclaimed Alma, extending her hand.

"A thousand, my dear Miss Maitland. Pray excuse me for giving your father the priority which, by virtue of your sex, belongs to you," said Noel, ready to sink on his knees in gratitude for their kind reception.

He noted with proud pleasure how the eyes of both father and daughter sparkled with a new-born life. It was his doing—his advent had inspired them with fresh hope and courage.

"We have often talked of you," said Mr. Maitland; "and I have regretted those words which meant nothing, but which drove you away. Yes, I have regretted them but once, and that has been ever since. You were foolish; I was thoughtless."

"And what will you say to me, when I tell you that I was quite nervous about coming down here? I thought you would turn me away, and I should go back rebuffed and crestfallen. I assure you, your kind reception has taken a great weight off my mind."

And then there was great rejoicing, and many ques-

tions were asked and answered. Mr. Maitland, formerly so taciturn, became quite loquacious, and even
hilarious, when Noel said,

"You must not reject the offer of my services; for
I want to settle down here in the country, and be your
bailiff, your steward, your head man. I will look after
the farm, and we will make it a prosperous undertaking.
I want no wages; only something to eat and drink, and
a truss of straw to lie upon."

"You must not estimate the resources of this establishment so meanly as that, Mr. Evander," said Alma,
with a laugh; "for I beg to state we have a sufficiency
of beds; and we brought our own linen with us, having
saved that from the wreck. If you prefer sleeping with
the cows and the pigs, of course we will place plenty
of clean straw at your disposal; for I believe it is the
fashion for every one down here to call his house Liberty Hall, and we will make no exception to so general
a rule."

Then they all laughed again, and at length Mr.
Maitland hit upon the palpable idea that Noel must
be hungry after his walk; and they went into the house.
The servant quickly placed a rabbit-pie on the table.
Alma drew some beer from a barrel with her own hands,
and placed it before Noel, who did justice to the hospitality of the owner of Woodbine.

Mr. Maitland would not let him out of his sight.
Noel's arrival was a real piece of good luck for him.
Now he saw a chance of a nice companion to go out
shooting, riding, or fishing with—now there would be
some one to play backgammon and chess with in the
evening.

The old gentleman took Noel by the arm, and said

he would show him the farm—Alma promising to get
tea ready by the time they returned in a couple of
hours. It was a long walk, but a very charming one.
Noel felt inexpressibly happy in the abnegation of self
he was about to practise; and Mr. Maitland was overjoyed to think that he had acquired a friend and a
companion.

The land was in a very neglected state; well stocked
with game, however—abounding with rabbits and wild-
fowl. The streams were full of fish, and there was
every prospect of good sport—of all kinds of sport, in
fact—from a solan goose to a king-fisher or water-wag-
tail, from a pheasant to a fieldfare.

Noel entered on his stewardship, and soon managed
to pick up the art of farming. He made the men work
hard, and do a good day's work for a fair day's pay.
He cropped the land, and looked after the live stock,
and created quite a sensation in the vicinity of Woodbine.

Was it not a strange fatality, however, that he
should always come in contact with Sir Charles Evander? He had not been in the country a week, before
he discovered that he lived close by and was at home.
Having made this discovery, he carefully avoided the
place, because he did not wish to meet him.

Yet what he strove to avoid came to pass.

He was on horseback one afternoon in the month of
September. The lane up which he was riding was very
narrow—so narrow, in fact, as to prevent two people
on horseback passing one another. All at once a man
appeared cantering up on a powerful gray cob.

"Go back! Go back, or jump the hedge!" shouted
Noel, thinking he had the right of way.

"Go back yourself !" was the churlish reply.

Noel reined-in his horse, and found himself face to face with the young baronet, who had come down for a fortnight to inform the pheasants, partridges, and game generally upon the estate that he was in the flesh still, and had not forgotten them.

Noel knew him, and bit his lip with vexation.

Nevertheless he was determined not to give way.

<hr />

CHAPTER XII.

A HEAVY BLOW.

"MAKE way there ! make way ! Do you know who I am ? If not, I shall have to teach you in a manner which will be more forcible than pleasant !" shouted Sir Charles Evander, considerably nettled at the attitude of resistance assumed by Noel.

"I know who you are ; but I'm sure I don't care," replied Noel, with as much insolence as he could infuse into his manner.

He knew perfectly well who Sir Charles was, and determined to defy him, which made him grow furious.

"You had best take care," Sir Charles said angrily, "or something unpleasant may happen. Do you intend to go back ?"

"I certainly shall not move an inch. I have come some distance up the lane ; you have only just entered it. If you were to go back a couple of dozen yards, the difficulty would be at an end. I have the right of way, and decidedly shall not go back."

" O, you won't, eh ?"

" I have told you so."

Sir Charles looked at Noel, and, in common phrase, took his measure. He was not quite sure whether he would be successful in a contest with him, and so he thought he would continue to bully him before he had recourse to force.

" Look here," he cried; " it's no use your being obstinate, because I could ride over you, if I chose."

" You'd better try it, then," was the loud and defiant answer.

Sir Charles found that he had for once met his match. He wished that he had not entered into an altercation with so resolute an opponent. He sat still on his horse's back, sulkily gnawing the end of his whip, wondering what it was best for him to do in order to extricate himself with credit from the dilemma in which he was.

Noel quietly took his pipe out of his pocket, then his pouch and fusee-box, charged the pipe, lighted the tobacco, and began to smoke placidly, as if he had made up his mind to stay where he was for some time.

" I know you," cried Sir Charles Evander; " and you shall repent this ; mark my words !"

Noel laughed sarcastically; and his antagonist, setting spurs to his horse, leapt a hedge, thus putting an unexpected end to the difficulty.

Soon afterwards he was seen cantering over some fallow land as quickly as the heavy nature of the ground would permit him.

For some little time Noel heard no more of Sir Charles; but one day he received a terrible proof of his malignant mind and vindictive memory. Mr. Maitland was under the impression that he had paid all his debts, and satisfied every claim against him. In this belief he was disastrously mistaken. He had been indebted, a few years back, to a wine-merchant, in the sum of a thousand pounds. The man disappeared. Some said he was dead, others that he had gone to America. Be that as it may, he returned to the scene of his former activity, and Sir Charles Evander happened to deal with him. The wine-merchant's name was Brooks, and he borrowed some money from Sir Charles, which he was unable to pay. In this emergency Sir Charles waited upon him, and looked over his books.

"What is this item?" asked Sir Charles, pointing to a debt marked 'doubtful.'

"That is a debt I have given up," replied the wine-merchant. "The money was owing me before I went away some years ago. It is yet within the statute of limitations; but the man has failed, and gone no one knows where."

"The name, I see, is Maitland. What Maitland is it?"

"You must have heard of him. A very rich man. Once he had a fine place in the country, and a grand house in Brunswick-square, Brighton."

"Ah, I think I remember the name. The man, as I suppose you are aware, is not worth a penny now."

"So I am given to understand."

"And in failing health."

"Indeed!" said the wine-merchant.

"I'll tell you what I'll do, though. I'll give you ten pounds for your debt."

"You will? Say twenty, and you shall have it."

"Fifteen. Split the difference, and say fifteen."

Upon this the bargain was struck.

The baronet gave a cheque for fifteen pounds for the debt, and went away conscious of his power over poor, ruined, broken-down Mr. Maitland.

He had discovered that Noel was domiciled in Mr. Maitland's house; and his own wit told him that he was an admirer of Alma, and that she looked favourably upon his suit.

Alma had always treated Sir Charles with a quiet scorn that had stung him to the quick. Here, then, was a famous opportunity of revenging himself upon Alma and Noel—he could kill both birds with one stone, and he did not shrink from doing it.

The very next day saw him in a lawyer's office.

Mr. Taper was a friend of his, and readily consented to make an application for the thousand pounds.

Imagine the consternation of Mr. Maitland when he opened Mr. Taper's letter at the breakfast-table.

When the postman arrived, Mr. Maitland was engaged in conversation with Noel respecting the improved state and condition of the farm, which, under Noel's energetic and sensible management, was increasing in value every day, and promising to become quite a profitable little property before long.

Mr. Taper wrote:

"Sir,—I am instructed by my client, Sir Charles Evander, to apply to you for payment of one thousand pounds—"

"Eh! what!" interjected the old gentleman; "I owe no thousand pounds. Some mistake—must be a mistake."

"This debt was originally contracted four years and a half ago. Perhaps it will be in your memory that

I

you owed a wine-merchant of the name of Brooks a thousand pounds—"

"Brooks! Why, the man's dead—at least, I always thought so."

"The debt has passed in the way of business to my client Sir Charles Evander, who is the holder for value; and I am instructed to say, that if the money be not paid to me at my office, Lincoln's-inn-fields, within one month from this day, proceedings to recover the same will be taken in one of her Majesty's courts of law.—I am, sir, yours obediently,   R. TAPER.

"To *Mr. Maitland.*"

"God bless me! What a blow! This is indeed un-expected—it is almost more than I can bear. My poor Alma, what will become of you?"

In reply to her father's piteous exclamation, Alma threw her arms around his neck, and kissed him ten-derly, mixing her tears with his.

"Never mind, my father," she said; "there is One above who will protect us. I can work, and will work, to keep you. If the worst comes to the worst, we shall have money enough to buy a sewing machine, and with that I can make a great deal, you know."

Alma was one of those sanguine young ladies who have a great idea of a sewing machine. They fancy that they can always make a certain sum every day by working for some shop, and that a machine will enable them to do wonders.

"We must sell our farm, my child, and what is there before us but starvation and the workhouse? The pro-spect is so dreary, that I dare not look it full in the face; I am turning coward in my old age."

Noel had refrained from saying anything until the

first burst of grief emanating from the father and daughter was past. When he thought he could with delicacy interfere, he said, "Perhaps Sir Charles, as an old friend, may be induced to take a more lenient view of the case. As he was so well and intimately acquainted with you in the days of your prosperity, he may be induced to take the interest of the debt instead of the principal."

"Friends!" cried the old man fiercely, "I have no friends. When I was rich, and had houses and lands, I had also friends in abundance; but now, as God is my witness, I do not know one man or woman who would go out of their way to give me the value of a five-pound note."

"At any rate, it would be worth your while, sir, to write to Sir Charles, and ask him if he will take annually five per cent on his debt."

After some conversation, Mr. Maitland, clinging like a drowning man to a straw, agreed to do as Noel suggested. The letter to the baronet was written, and this was the gist of his reply:

"I regret sincerely that it is out of my power to listen to your application. The matter is out of my hands. My creditors are pressing me for money, and my mother will not come to my assistance; in this dilemma I am obliged to draw upon all the resources I have. May I ask, that any future communication you have to make may be addressed to Mr. Taper, of Lincoln's-inn-fields, who is my solicitor, and who acts for me in this painful matter?"

It was clear that this epistle had been dictated by Mr. Taper. It had more of his smooth Ionic style than of the rough Doric of the baronet.

"Well, well; God's will be done!" said Mr. Maitland, when he saw that all hope was gone. "In three weeks' time or thereabouts we shall be sold up, and have to beg our bread from door to door."

"O no, papa; it is not so bad as that," said Alma. "Have I not told you I can work?"

"And I too, dear sir, can and will work for you," exclaimed Noel enthusiastically. "You do not suppose that I will desert you because you are poor?"

"I have no claim upon your services, Noel. It is noble of you to say that you will work for us, but you are sacrificing your future. I cannot allow you to do that; it is not right," said Mr. Maitland reflectively.

"I have no father, sir. Let me look upon you as one; let me regard Miss Maitland as a dear sister."

The old man wrung his hands silently; a lump rose in his throat, and he could not speak. Fortunately his agitation prevented him from noticing the flush which appeared on his daughter's face as she encountered Noel's gaze, burning and ardent, fixed upon her.

The month passed, the money was not paid, and Sir Charles Evander ordered an action at law, by serving the owner of Woodbine Farm with a writ. When Mr. Maitland received the fatal piece of paper beginning with "Victoria, by the grace of God," he trembled violently, threw up his hands, and cried in a heart-broken voice, "All is over!"

CHAPTER XIII.

PRIDE AND POVERTY.

NOEL thought, that in the midst of the poverty and distress which had unexpectedly fallen on Mr. Maitland he might successfully urge his suit to Alma. When Mr. Maitland was prosperous he was very proud. As long as the workhouse did not yawn for him with open doors, he would have sooner seen his daughter dead than the wife of an obscure plebeian. So, after much thought and deliberation, Noel determined to speak to Alma, and tell her, with all the passionate earnestness of which he was capable, that he loved her, and would be proud and happy to make her his wife.

Alma was particularly enamoured of a shady place beneath an aged oak-tree which overshadowed the cool pellucid waters of a lake. Here she would sit for hours, reading a favourite book, or feeding the mandarin ducks and black geese, who had learned to love her.

Noel found her in this shady spot, whither she had come after breakfast. Tears were running down her cheeks. She was bidding the solitude an adieu; for in a short time she would have to quit it, and go to the dingy and smoky precincts of the city.

She looked up like a startled fawn when the form of the intruder was visible. His presence did not appear to be unwelcome, though she said rather coldly, "I thought you were with my father, Noel."

"I have left him writing a letter; and fancying you would be here, I took the liberty of following you, as I have something to say which is better said when we are by ourselves and secure from interruption."

"What can you have to say to me of so private and confidential a nature?" she asked, looking very much confused, and blushing like a rose at dawn of day.

Noel sat down at the margin of the lake, a few feet from the camp-stool upon which the idol of his heart was sitting, and amused himself for a brief space before he replied by throwing pebbles into the water, and watching the eddies made by the little stones.

"It is sad that Mr. Maitland should be compelled to leave Woodbine," he exclaimed at length; "he had made up his mind to spend the last days of his life here. I wish I could avert the inevitable doom; but unhappily I am powerless."

"What puzzles me is the vindictiveness displayed by Sir Charles Evander," said Alma.

"That is easily explained."

"Is it so? Then you are cleverer than I am."

"Shall I tell you my explanation of what perplexes you? You cannot have forgotten that my cousin Sir Charles hates me, and has paid you great attention. You not only discouraged, but snubbed him. He thinks that by making you entirely dependent upon your own exertions for your support, he will break your spirit, and that when he proposes to marry you, his advances may be met in a far different way to what they were the last time he spoke to you upon the delicate subject of love."

"Do you think so?" said Alma, with sparkling eyes. "If so, I will speedily undeceive him. If I were as poor as Job, I would not listen to a word of love from him for the world. Why should I give my hand where my heart can never accompany it? No, no! He cannot think so poorly of me as to suppose that poverty will make me sell my independence."

" Have you never thought of love, Miss Maitland ?" asked Noel.

" N—o," she replied hesitatingly.

" Ah, how happy you must be ! I wish I could say the same, for I have never known a moment's peace since I gave my heart away."

" And pray who is the divinity to whom you gave it ?"

" Cannot you guess ?"

" I guess ! How should I ? What do I know about your private affairs ?" she cried, with a light laugh.

He was silent, and threw more pebbles into the lake.

" Come, tell me who the lady is ? Open confession is good for the soul, you know," she said, trying to appear calm and serene.

He turned his honest lustrous eyes full upon her, and said, " You have asked me for the confession, so you must not blame me if—if——"

" Well, speak out. Do not hesitate. I promise not to blame you under any circumstances."

" In that case I have no hesitation in admitting that the lady—the divinity—is—*yourself*."

" Me ! O, how ridiculous ! Surely you are joking, Mr. Evander."

She called him Mr. Evander, whereas he had been Noel a few moments ago.

" Joking !" he repeated, rising to his feet, and seizing her hand with every demonstration of the most loyal and ardent affection. " I declare most solemnly that I was never more in earnest in my life than I am at this moment. O, Alma ! dear, dear Alma ! if you only knew how I love you, and how I have loved you ever since the first day I had the happiness of meeting you, I feel convinced you would pity me, if nothing else. I would not utter my love to you in the days of your prosperity, because I feared you might think me mercenary, and that I loved your father's money-bags better than I did your lovely self; but now, now, when your future looks dim and louring, and dark clouds are gathering over the horizon of your life, I venture to speak of my love, hoping that you will tell me I am not hateful to you."

"Inessa La Beata told me something of this," said Alma thoughtfully, as the young man, exhausted by passionate declamation, desisted, and gazed so lovingly upon her, that it seemed a harsh answer would be instant death to him.

"You know my father, and you know his disposition as well as I do," she resumed; "he is very particular."

"I am sorry that it should be so," replied Noel; "for I own frankly, I am not well off, though my relations are rich. I may be able to boast of good blood; but, on the other hand, I have no money."

"I fear that papa will hardly forgive you," said Alma, shaking her head; "he wants a rich husband for me."

"But you—do you, dearest Alma, share your father's prejudices?"

"No, I do not; for I think them exceedingly silly and illiberal."

"May I interpret that in my favour?" asked Noel. "Pray let me think, that if you do not love me as I love you, at least you look upon me as a friend—as one whom you may love in time."

"You must pardon me for 'not giving you a full and decisive answer just now, for your confession of love comes so suddenly upon me, that I have had no time to think."

"Will you tell me one thing?" asked Noel piteously. "I don't know whether I have any right to ask it, but I feel impelled to do so. Will you tell me, that if you cannot marry me, you will never marry any one else?"

"I will," she replied, returning his manly grasp with a gentle pressure of her lilliputian hand; "if I do not marry you, I will—what shall I say?—die an old maid."

Here she smiled faintly, and Noel was transported with joy. He had succeeded much better than he had anticipated. He had made an impression upon Alma, and she loved him. That was quite sufficient. He could live a lifetime upon that sweet assurance. She had kindled the spark of hope in his breast, and fanned it with a gentle breeze, which made it burn brightly.

In the height of his enthusiasm he raised her hand to his lips, and kissed it with such rapture as he never knew before.

Yet the serpent came into his Eden. He had built himself a paradise out of very commonplace materials; still it was a paradise, and he would have defied any mortal to prove it otherwise. It is not often that men enjoy such happiness as Noel enjoyed for a brief space. It is said, that when joy is very great, it is too ecstatic to last. So it was in his case.

A harsh voice fell upon his ear; and, stupefied as with the sound of a thunderclap, he heard Mr. Mait-

land, who had come unexpectedly upon the lovers, exclaim,

"This conduct, sir, is not only cowardly and un-
gentlemanly, but intolerable. I have been an unwilling listener to what has just taken place between my
daughter and yourself; and I have no hesitation in saying, that the behaviour on your part that I have this
day witnessed is very disgraceful."

"Really, Mr.——"

"Hear me out, sir; your turn will come presently. Does it follow, that because I am poor and
in misfortune, I am to give my daughter's hand to
any penniless adventurer who may do her the honour
to fall in love with her? If you have been of service
to me lately, have I not taken you in, and boarded
and lodged you? The obligation is by no means one-
sided. I could see through your object when you first
followed me into the country. I knew as well as anybody that you were not the sort of man to devote your
time, in a 'friendly' way, to me or to any one else;
but though I deemed you mercenary, I had no suspicion
that your audacity would fly to such height as it has
done."

Noel was very much hurt at this cruel speech.
Mr. Maitland was blinded by passion, or he would not
have made use of the intemperate and unjust language
which had fallen from his lips.

To his credit be it said, Noel did not reply in
the same strain ; he was more hurt than angry, and
kept his temper excellently ; in short, he preserved
an admirable self-possession throughout the distressing
scene which ensued.

"Now that you have abused my hospitality, and

shown me what a viper I have cherished," continued
Mr. Maitland, "I have only to order you to leave my
house and quit these premises, which are yet mine,
though God only knows how long they may remain so.
Go, sir; go at once, lest I be tempted to call one of the
farm-servants to eject you forcibly, as you richly deserve to be ejected."

"I will go, sir," said Noel sadly; "though for your
own sake, and for that of Miss Maitland, I could wish
you to see my conduct by a different light. I am innocent of any intention of insulting you, or of being
ungrateful. I appreciate your kindness, though you
fail to appreciate mine. Some day, perhaps, the scales
may fall from your eyes, and you will be prepared to
admit yourself in the wrong. At present I can only
regret that you are so obstinate in viewing what has
occurred through a false medium."

"Will you go, sir? The air is contaminated by
your presence!" vociferated Mr. Maitland.

"O, papa, do not be so violent!" said Alma.

"Are you too in rebellion against me? If so, you
had better go with him."

Alma covered her face with her hands, and began
to cry.

"Go, sir!" again shouted Mr. Maitland. "You
are a wretch, for you have endeavoured to steal my
daughter from me. She is the support of my age—
my lamb, my pet-lamb—and you would steal her; but I
have thwarted you. Yes, yes; the old man was not
such a fool as you took him to be."

Seeing that further expostulation would be useless,
Noel did not attempt to say a word. He walked quietly
away, and by the evening of that day was in Brighton.

CHAPTER XIV.

A SCENE AT MUTTON'S.

IT was again the season at Brighton, when Noel, driven forth by Mr. Maitland, sought the favourite watering-place. He was burning with resentment at the harsh injustice he had received, but he determined to in no way reproach the father of the girl he passionately loved. It was with a vague hope that he should meet with Sir Charles Evander, his cousin, that he went to Brighton; and he was also influenced in favour of the queen of watering-places by a wish to be near Alma. It was not impossible that he might effect a reconciliation; but his first wish was to have an interview with Sir Charles, and publicly demand an explanation from him of his vindictiveness towards himself and the Maitlands. He knew that Sir Charles was at Brighton always in the season: and rumour, which is ever busy with the names of those who are prominent in society, had said that Lady Carisbrook was also there.

Noel was far from being well off, but he had sufficient money to pay for his pressing necessities; and he waited, Micawber-like, to see if something would not turn up, and resolved to rack his brains day by day to see if he could hit on some expedient of gaining sufficient at least to live upon.

Alma was ever present to his imagination; and one morning, when walking slowly along the beach, his country attire not fitting him to mix with the gay promenaders on the West Pier, he was so lost in admiration of the charms of his mistress, that he ran up against a gentleman named Clements, a local solicitor, an agreeable fellow, who had transacted some business for Noel a short time back, which had made them acquainted.

" Thank you," exclaimed Mr. Clements, gasping for the breath which Noel had nearly knocked out of him ; " it is lucky for you that I am not a post."

" There is no post after breakfast till twelve, and consequently I did not—"

" Don't make a bad pun," interrupted Mr. Clements, cutting Noel's facetious attempt very short. " Let me take your arm. These stones tire me. We will get on the Parade, and you shall tell me all about your retirement from the farm, for I have heard something about your disagreement with Mr. Maitland. Don't think me impertinent, but I take an interest in you."

Noel looked at his coat in a deprecating manner, which was perfectly understood by Mr. Clements, who, having an overcoat on his arm, made him put it on, saying, " Two letters would have described your condition just now—C. D. But I have made you all right. Don't thank me. Perhaps you will be able to do something for me some day."

" Thanks," replied Noel. " But the state of my pockets is answerable for my condition, and that can also be described by two letters—M. T."

Mr. Clements laughed, and said, " We must try and remedy that. If I had seen you a month ago, I could have given you a berth in my office ; but Mr. Maitland, though not exactly rude, does not make any secret of his dislike to solicitors. He only makes use of the law when compelled. But I always drink his health, for I think he is a good friend to the lawyers, or will be some day ; for if he has anything to leave, he will be sure to make his own will, and then his heirs will have a poor chance."

"You mean, litigation will ensue, and the lawyers will get all," said Noel.

"Certainly. Poor fellow, I am sorry for him. His was a great loss. The change in his position was enough to kill him."

"It has made a great alteration."

"Is his daughter good to him?"

"Good! She is an angel, sir,—an angel incarnate. There never was such a dear creature, sir."

"That will do," said Mr. Clements gravely. "I don't want to know any more about your quarrel with Mr. Maitland. You made love to the girl, and he politely told you to go about your business, eh?"

"I should not have cared, if he had been polite, but he was not commonly civil," answered Noel, who could not help smiling at the lawyer's quickness of perception.

"Ah, well," replied Mr. Clements, "it is a great worry to be crossed in your first love; but it may be all right yet, if the girl herself does not object to you. The father's pride has seldom much effect upon the daughter, who, when opposed, is generally all the more obstinate, and determined to gratify her own inclinations. Perhaps I can help you; at all events, I'll try. What do you say to driving a quill in my office at thirty shillings a-week for a month or two? That won't hurt your pride, will it?"

"My dear sir!" was all Noel could say.

"That's settled. That's a bargain, then? Come over to Mutton's and have a mutton-pie. I don't mean anything made of sheep, but a thing with turkey and truffles, and all that," continued the facetious lawyer.

"Don't look as if you were afraid of me. A glass of wine and a snack will do you good. You mustn't mope because you have lost your lady-love for a time."

All the current of Noel's being set in towards his generous friend, and he pressed his hand in token of his appreciation of his kindness.

" I cannot thank you," he said.

" Don't want you to," answered Mr. Clements. " I know how you feel. You could sing a song in the street, or stand on your head in a corner with your back against the wall. It's the way with young men when they have not had too much bad luck, and they get a turn of good. Singing is a capital let-off when the steam of prosperity gets up. I don't know a better vent. An old widow lady died the other day—a client —and left me a thousand pounds as a legacy. I began to sing directly I heard of it. Perhaps you were not aware that it was one of my accomplishments?"

Noel said he was not.

"O, yes. I sing as well as most men in Europe. I'll prove it to you by strict logic. Refer to Whately, if you have any doubts. Most men in Europe do not sing well. I am an average singer; therefore I sing as well as most men in Europe."

Laughing again, Noel felt his spirits rise. His meeting with the lawyer was really a piece of unexpected luck. They reached Mutton's, and were entering arm-in-arm, when a beggar pushed the lawyer, and asked an alms. The lawyer annoyed, said brusquely,

" You had better ask for manners than money, my good fellow."

" I asked for what I thought you had the most of," answered the beggar.

"By Jove, that's good! that deserves half-a-sovereign; and you shall have it, if I have to go without my lunch," cried the solicitor admiringly.

He gave the man half-a-sovereign in acknowledgment of his ready wit; and the fellow, pocketing the coin, walked off, after thanking the donor for his munificence.

There were several people at Mutton's whom Mr. Clements knew, and he soon got into conversation. A lady and gentleman, sitting at the same table as Noel and his friend, were delighted to see the lawyer. These were Sir Philip Dando and his wife. Dando was known in Brighton, where he had been a resident for some years, as a close-fisted curmudgeon, and his wife was not much better. They were always quarrelling, and did not wait till they got home, washing their dirty linen in public as often as not.

Sir Philip had a great idea of getting advice from professional men for nothing. He would ask them a variety of questions bearing upon his affairs in a casual sort of way, and make mental notes of the answers. He was subject to attacks of the gout, and was once much offended because a well-known Brighton practitioner in reply to his query, "Can you give me a cure for the gout?" had replied in the words of Abernethy, "Live upon sixpence a-day, and earn it." The Dandos had a daughter named Angelina, and she became the laughing-stock of all Brighton, through a remark made to her by her mother, which some one overheard, as well as Miss Dando's reply.

Mrs. W., the famous stockbroker's wife, had given a ball, to which every one who was anybody was invited. It was a grand affair, intended to eclipse one

which Mrs. Leo S. had given a short time previously.
The Dandos were there; and Lady Dando seeing her
daughter walk languidly through a quadrille with one
who seemed an eligible *parti*, ventured to say to her in
a sort of stage-whisper, which was loud enough to be
overheard, " A little more animation, my dear: vivacity
is everything." To which the prudent Angelina replied,
while the sides were going through their part of the
quadrille, " Leave me, please, mamma, to manage my
own business. Do you want me to dance myself out of
curl, and for a married man?" This altered the complexion of affairs at once. The mamma said, "No, my
dear ; forgive me. I did not know who or what your
partner was."

This story became a great joke, and the Dandos
furnished amusing conversation for many a drawing-
room that winter.

" Now, Mr. Clements," said Sir Philip, " I have
often given you my opinion on things in general, and
I want yours on a particular point of law."

" Excuse me, Sir Philip," answered the lawyer;
" but I never had any opinion of you in my life."

With a miserable attempt at a smile, Sir Philip
Dando replied, " That is, I believe, actionable. However, I don't mind you. You will have your joke, if
you lose your friend. Now tell me: suppose I lend a
man five pounds without any security, what——"

" My dear good sir," interrupted the lawyer, "don't
please bother me with hypothetical cases."

" But this is true."

" Impossible, I'm sure, Sir Philip ; the sky will fall,
and people catch larks, before you lend any one five
pounds without security."

K

"I tell you I did," said Sir Philip testily.

"Then all I can say is, you were a greater fool than I took you to be," replied the lawyer bluntly. "Don't be offended. Come to my office to-morrow, and I daresay, if you like to spend five pounds and throw it after the first, I may succeed in getting a county-court judgment against your debtor ; but as to the money, I really cannot hazard an opinion. It's awfully difficult to get money back when you've once parted with it."

"My dear," said Lady Dando, who had taken no part in this conversation, "I am waiting for you."

"Don't you see I am engaged in business?" replied Sir Philip, who was in what his wife called a 'grumpy' humour; adding to Clements *sotto voce,* "Marriage is the churchyard of love."

"Is it?" cried her ladyship, whose quick ears detected the remark; "then all I can say is, the men are the gravediggers."

Sir Philip, dreading a matrimonial disturbance before the lawyer and the crowd of people at Mutton's, got up, said good-bye in a hurry, and paying at the counter, gave his arm to his affectionate spouse, and rated her soundly all the way home ; she retorting with no want of energy, until they were quite ready to throw one another into the waves of the salt, salt sea.

"That is Dando's second wife; and, by George, he has got a treasure in her !" observed Clements.

"I don't believe in second love," replied Noel.

"Why not? Suppose you buy a pound of sugar; is not it sweet? and when that is gone, and you buy another, won't the second be sweet too?"

"That is sophistical reasoning. For my part, I am

sure I could never, never love any one but Alma Maitland."

Noel sighed deeply as he uttered these words.

"That is because you are bitten with your first love. It's bad, I know; but it is not an incurable disease. Shall I tell you how to be happy in life? Never vex yourself about what you can't help ; and secondly, never vex yourself about what you can help."

"I should want a mind of fifty philosopher-power to follow your advice," replied Noel smiling.

A gentleman at this moment pushed past Noel, and rudely jogged his elbow, without making any apology, which caused him to look up.

"Sir Charles Evander," exclaimed Noel.

"I do not know you, sir," replied the young baronet, whose face was flushed as if from drinking.

"But you do know me, and I will force you to confess it; and I will make you tell me here, before you leave this room, why you persecute me and my friends in the relentless manner which has characterised your conduct lately," cried Noel spiritedly.

Evander would have passed on, but Noel seemed determined to follow him, and he was averse to a scene which could not fail to be disagreeable in its details.

"What do you want?" he said, twirling his moustache, which bristled like that of an angry cat.

"Sit down here by my side," replied Noel, "and I will tell you. My presence will not contaminate you," he added, as Sir Charles hesitated. "I am your cousin, after all, if I am poor—our fathers were brothers, you know. This gentleman is my good friend Mr. Clements."

"I really don't want to know your friends. It is

bad enough to be forced into holding intercourse with you. It may be an honour to be acquainted with them, but it is not one of which I am ambitious."

This nettled the lawyer, who instantly said, "Although a stranger to you, sir, I am well known in this town, and I shall not permit myself to be insulted by you. I demand an apology, or at least an explanation."

"I have none to give you," replied Sir Charles Evander coolly. "If you will let me settle my affairs with this headstrong young man first, I daresay I shall be able to attend to you. It is too bad that I should be bullied by two people at once."

Mr. Clements bit his lip, and waited while Noel went again to the charge. Sir Charles Evander listened complacently, not interrupting him by a word or a sign.

"You remember, Sir Charles," said Noel, "that we first met on the Parade, when Lord Carisbrook committed the cowardly assault on you for some wrong he alleged you had done him. I went with you to your hotel, and told you that I was your cousin, that I was poor, and should feel thankful if you would assist me, or put me in the way of doing something for myself. You requested me to call again. I did so, and you refused to see me, eventually giving me a few pounds. Since then you have not lost an opportunity of insulting me. You find me domiciled with kind friends, and you endeavour to ruin them. Why do you do this? What is the reason of your hostility? What have I done to deserve such treatment? If I were a stranger, it would be cruel; but to a cousin like myself it is monstrous."

"Very well said, young man," exclaimed a voice behind them.

It was Dr. Rox, who had unexpectedly made his appearance on the scene. Evander was somewhat embarrassed to see him, but he held out his hand, saying, "How do, Doctor? you are in time to assist at an important family council, which has been forced on me very much against my will."

"So be it. I will preside at this council; and perhaps no one has a greater right to do so than myself," answered Dr. Rox, sitting down.

At this juncture Sir Charles Evander, unobserved by any one, extended his arm, and let a purse belonging to him slip into Noel's coat-pocket, which gaped conveniently to receive it. What his object in committing this extraordinary act was, will be seen shortly.

CHAPTER XV

THE LOST PURSE.

"You have heard what this gentleman has said. I do not dispute his relationship to me; I do not question his right to appeal to me; nor am I about to reproach him for stopping me publicly to present again his petition as it were," exclaimed Evander. "His observations all amount to one thing: Give me money. Now I do deny his right to expect me to contribute to his support. If his father has not left him well off, is it my business? If the world will not recognise his merit, and refuses to support him, is it my fault? Am I to blame?"

"You are labouring under a misapprehension," said Mr. Clements.

"Am I indeed? I shall be thankful if you will correct me," answered Evander.

"You accuse my friend here—Mr. Noel Evander—of what, in fact, amounts to genteel begging. You are wrong: he wants no money from you. If I understand him rightly, it is a request for justice that he made to you."

"I am glad to hear it; for it would have annoyed me considerably to be obliged to refuse him a second time. Let him understand, once for all, that I cannot, and will not contribute to the support of poor relations."

"I have taken him into my service, and I will answer for it that his wants are provided for in such a way that he will not trouble you," said Mr. Clements.

"It is fortunate that he has found so generous a patron."

"Mr. Clements is right," said Noel. "I want nothing from my cousin in the shape of money. All I want him to do is to cease from persecuting Mr. Maitland. Sir Charles has lately bought-up an old debt of Mr. Maitland's, and he is in danger of being thrown upon the world, and having the fragment of property belonging to him sold by auction, simply because a new and vindictive creditor arises in the person of my cousin. Let him persecute me, if he will; but do not let him visit my friends with his displeasure."

"This is ridiculous," replied Evander. "If I am put upon my defence to this absurd charge, I can only say that I bought the debt for its full market value; and if Mr. Maitland does not pay it, he must take the consequences. I know nothing about his position. We were friends once, but his poverty has of course altered that. I cannot afford to know a poor man, who is out of society : still, I am told that he is not so poor as he has been represented."

"You are misinformed," exclaimed Noel eagerly. "The poor old gentleman has nothing but the proceeds of the little bit of land of which you threaten to deprive him. You are rich, and I implore you to give up your claim against him, or at least to let him have time to get the money together for you to spend upon your fashionable vices."

"I spend my income as I choose, and shall not consult you," answered Evander. "It is useless to urge me further. You may go on talking from Genesis to Revelation, my good fellow, and be only wasting your time."

He rose, and felt in his pockets for his purse, but could not find it.

"Dear me," he added, "this is odd and embarrassing. I was going to give you a sovereign to drink my health, but I find my purse is gone."

"These insults, Sir Charles—" began Noel, when his cousin interrupted him, saying,

"Do not let us have any virtuous indignation, if you please, or I shall think you want to prevent me making a search for my purse."

"Preposterous!" answered Noel. "You will say next that I have taken it."

"It would not surprise me in the least," he exclaimed: adding, as he saw the threatening demeanour of Noel, "I did not mean to rile your Tom Sayers, and rouse your fighting instinct. Take care what you do. For an assault I should prosecute you. Feel in your pockets, and see if you have taken up my purse by mis-

take. People in your position do make blunders sometimes between ' mine and thine.' "

An angry flush rose to Noel's cheeks, as he almost
involuntarily inserted his hands in his pockets to dis-
prove the charge. But what was his amazement when
he discovered the missing purse in the right-hand pocket
of his coat!—that coat which Mr. Clements had given
him. Holding it up, he exclaimed, " Here is a purse
which does not belong to me, but which I expect is
Mr. Clements', as he just now gave me the coat I am
wearing."

" No, my friend; that is not my property," said Mr.
Clements, regarding him curiously.

" The excuse is ingenious, I will admit," said Sir
Charles Evander, with a smile of triumph ; " but I will
put an end to all doubts by saying that the purse is
mine ; and I declare that it was safely deposited within
my pocket when I entered this shop."

A solemn silence reigned for a brief space ; every
one was astounded.

Noel was the first to speak. " Appearances are
against me," he said in a tone of great distress; " but I
will swear that I am innocent of any thought of steal-
ing my cousin's purse. I never dreamt of such a thing ;
such an act is utterly foreign to all my antecedents, and
I know no more than a baby how it came where it has
been found."

" I beg to assure you that I had no participation in
the act," exclaimed Mr. Clements, who was getting
alarmed.

" Did I say you had, my good sir ?" replied Evander.
" Wait till you are accused. Remember, he who excuses
himself,—you know the rest."

"In what way shall you proceed?" inquired Dr. Rox, who had up to this time been a silent spectator of the scene.

"At present I can scarcely determine," said Evander. "If my cousin will give me an address where I shall be able to find him during the next three days, I shall be satisfied not to press the charge at present."

Noel hastily wrote down the address of his lodgings, and handed it to Sir Charles. "Here is my present address," he said. "Perhaps I may add that of Mr. Clements' offices."

"Not with my permission," hastily exclaimed the lawyer. "I—I must recall my promise to you. This business has an ugly look. You need not call upon me; as I shall fill up the vacant berth in my office in some other way."

Sir Charles Evander's face was illuminated with a smile of fiendish malignity. He had, indeed, triumphed beyond his expectations; for he had ruined Noel's character in the estimation of one who had been, and wished to show himself, his good friend.

"As you please, sir," answered Noel, with a dignity that was grand in that trying hour. "I will repeat that I am innocent; and I doubt not that God, in his own good time, will enable me to prove it. Think injuriously of me, if you will. I thank you for your professions of regard. Stay one moment," he added, as the lawyer, after bowing to Sir Charles and Dr. Rox, was going away. "This is your coat. Take it with you. If I have not your friendship, I will not receive your charity."

So saying, he divested himself of the garment, and threw it gently over the lawyer's arm, who departed with it. True, Noel stood revealed in all the shabbiness of

his poverty; but he felt prouder than if he had just been
"turned out" by the best Brighton tailor.

When Mr. Clements took his departure, Sir Charles
Evander rose, yawned, and said to the doctor, " Are you
disposed for a stroll ?"

" Not at present," replied Dr. Rox.

" O, pray don't make any favour of it," answered
Evander, with his usual insolence ; " I can do very well
without you."

The Doctor regarded him angrily, and watched him
till he left the shop. Then, turning to Noel, he exclaimed, " You are the son, I presume, of the late Sir
Harold Evander's brother, whose name was George
Evander?"

" I am," answered Noel.

" It is well we have met. I can serve you."

" First of all, sir, tell me if you believe me guilty
of the offence my cousin imputes to me."

" I do not. It is best to be on your guard against
him, though ; for he is capable of going to great lengths,
and you have much to fear from him. I can befriend
you, and I have every disposition to do so."

" I am sure that I feel very grateful for your kind
consideration," replied Noel.

" Don't alarm yourself in the least about the threats
of your cousin. Calm yourself, and go on with the
repast that he so inopportunely interrupted."

" I can eat nothing more, thank you."

" Drink a glass of wine. I will order it. You stand
in need of it, to keep up your spirits. I am a doctor ;
and you know that medical men are supreme, and must
not be contradicted."

Noel smiled faintly, and drank some sherry which

the Doctor ordered, and in compliance with a request which Dr. Rox made, he gave him an outline of his history, concealing nothing.

"Very well," said Dr. Rox; "you are good and virtuous, while Evander is bad and vicious. He must be punished, and you rewarded. Fortunately I can act now," he added, as if to himself, "for my dear old friend, Lady Evander, died last night in London.

"Died! Is Sir Charles's mother dead?"

"Yes."

"And he does not know it?"

"The news has not yet reached him; but he will hear of the melancholy event when he reaches his hotel. It is I who have brought the news, which will be welcome enough to him, for he has no heart; and as he has been obliged to pension his mother for some years, he will look upon her demise as a fortunate occurrence for him. Give me your address, so that I may know where to find you at a moment's notice. Do not leave Brighton in consequence of your cousin's hostility to you. I will protect not only you, but your friends the Maitlands also. Have you any money?"

"But little," answered Noel; "still I cannot permit myself to trespass upon your goodnature."

"Stuff and nonsense!" cried the Doctor. "Here is a note for ten pounds; when you have money in your pocket you can generally keep your courage up; if not, you are different from the majority of mankind."

Noel took the money with many protestations of gratitude, and gave the Doctor the address of the house in which he had taken lodgings; and Dr. Rox, walking to the door with him, paid what he owed for the wine, and shaking him cordially by the hand left him.

Events succeeded one another with great rapidity in his chequered career, and he scarcely knew what would befall him next. He bore a brave heart, however, and with the sanguine spirit of faith hoped for the best.

It was nevertheless with some annoyance that he, a few days afterwards, read in a local journal the following announcement:

"*Shilton, Sussex.* — *The contents of Woodbine Farm, comprising Household Furniture and Live and Dead Farming Stock.*

"Mr. Jacobson will sell by auction, on the premises, Woodbine Farm, Shilton, near Michester, on Sept. 29th, at eleven for twelve o'clock, the whole of the Household Furniture, and Live and Dead Farming Stock and Effects, including oak dining-room furniture, walnut-wood drawing-room suite and bed-room furniture, two horses, a well-built phaeton, Scotch cart, a set of nearly new double harness, a set of single ditto, two milch and in-calf cows, two pigs, thirty lambs, a retriever and a pointer, a quantity of poultry, and other effects; two stacks of prime meadow hay.—On view this day and morning of sale. Catalogues may be had at the principal inns in the neighbourhood; and at the Auctioneer's Offices, James-street, Brighton.

Mr. Maitland had evidently acted as he imagined he would. He had unreservedly placed his property—such as he had left—in his creditors' hands, that is to say, he had gone to Sir Charles Evander's attorney, and telling him he could not resist the justice of the claim which was really substantially made, because he had owed the wine-merchant the money applied for, and he unreservedly placed himself in his hands. This was, indeed, the true version of the case, as Noel afterwards ascertained. Sir Charles had ordered Mr. Maitland to be proceeded against rigorously, intending to apply to the Squire at the proper time for his daughter's hand ; and Mr. Maitland had gone to the solicitor, Mr. Taper, and given up everything. When this was communicated to Sir Charles, he lost no time in proceeding to the little farm.

Noel remained day after day waiting for news from Dr. Rox, unable to help his friend Mr. Maitland, longing to see Alma, and dreading some hostile proceeding on the part of his cold-hearted and unprincipled cousin, Sir Charles Evander.

CHAPTER XVI.

SIR CHARLES EVANDER MAKES LOVE.

IT was a fine autumn morning when Sir Charles Evander rode over to the farm to have an interview with Mr. Maitland, whose integrity he could not help admiring. The sun shone gaily over hill and dale, and the freshness of the air gave an exhilaration to the spirits. Mr. Maitland was at home when Sir Charles arrived, and received him with civility, not unmixed with hope. He thought that he had come to bring him tidings which would allow him to remain in the farmhouse on some reasonable terms. It was hard to lose the only bit of property he had left, and to be obliged to quit the pleasant spot in which he had fondly hoped to spend the remainder of his days in the agreeable and congenial society of his loved daughter. Sir Charles had been shown into the best room at the farmhouse, and Mr. Maitland welcomed him as we have said, with urbanity, but waited for him to speak.

" This is a disagreeable business which my solicitor writes me about," exclaimed Evander, with a hypocritical pretence of regret. " I have a claim against you, Mr. Maitland, as you know. A wine-merchant with whom you had once dealt owed me some money, and I took his claim upon you as a satisfaction of my debt, never dreaming for a moment that you could not satisfy it."

" I am prepared to do so, Sir Charles," said the old gentleman.

" By the sacrifice of your property?"

" That is the only way in which I can satisfy it, and I believe it is your wish that pressure should be put upon me to make me give up my farm."

" Pressure!" said Evander ; "an honest man should require no pressing to give another that which is his due."

" You are right. Pardon me for the expression ; I will correct it," replied Mr. Maitland. " It is your desire that your solicitor should obtain the money. I believe you will receive it shortly. Need we prolong this interview ?"

" With your kind permission."

Mr. Maitland bowed.

" My solicitor would not have received instructions from me to take proceedings against you," continued Sir Charles, " had I not myself been terribly pressed for money. Misfortunes never come singly, they say. I have just lost my mother, and I find that she was much involved. All claims against her I shall have to pay. In addition to this, a company, in which I am a shareholder has just become insolvent, and I lose heavily. I was informed that you were well off—that is to say, you could easily pay the thousand pounds. If I had not been worried for money myself, and full of a strong belief of your solvency, I should not have proceeded to extremities. I hope you fully understand that."

"I believe I do," answered Mr. Maitland, drily.

"It is impossible to praise you too highly for the splendid way in which you have behaved. Your conduct has been really magnificent; for, without any legal process, you have placed everything in the hands of my man of business, so I am told, to satisfy the debt."

"Your information is correct."

"It is very much to be regretted that we cannot settle this affair in an amicable manner," said Sir Charles.

"No one would be more happy than myself to do so," rejoined Mr. Maitland. "Can you submit any proposition to me which it is at all likely I can entertain?"

"I have for some time—it is useless to make a secret of it any longer," said Sir Charles Evander, in some slight confusion—"I—I have and do love your daughter, Mr. Maitland."

"Love Alma! love my daughter," cried the father. "Pray excuse any little agitation I may betray, but this announcement is so totally unexpected, that, upon my word, it nearly takes away my breath. Will you tell me if Alma—that is to say Miss Maitland—has any idea of the attachment you have just avowed?"

"I believe not, unless she has been able to guess

my secret from my behaviour to her when we have
been together. I have never spoken of love to her."

"In that case, you will, I fear, have a difficult task
to make any impression upon her."

"Have I your permission to make the attempt?"

"Certainly. I shall not put any constraint upon
my daughter. If you tell her you love her, which you
have my perfect permission to do, and she accepts you
as her affianced husband, I will wish you both joy."

"That is all I ask," said Sir Charles. "But why
do you anticipate any difficulty, may I inquire?"

"By all means. I like to be perfectly candid and
open with every one, and it will give me especial pleasure to be so with you to-day. Alma has formed an
attachment for a fellow who has grossly abused my
confidence. You cautioned me against him some time
ago. He is a namesake of yours, and your cousin—so
he alleges. He made love to my daughter, and I detected him in the act of offering her his hand and heart
in the most romantic manner, and——"

"You banished him?"

"Forthwith. He did not enter my house again."

"I commend you very much for your conduct. Your
child is worthy of a better fate," answered Sir Charles.

"If you will have the goodness to wait here a short
time, Sir Charles, I will send my daughter into the
house. She is now in the poultry-yard, bidding good-
bye to her pets. We will have an early dinner, and
you will have an opportunity of speaking to her on the
subject nearest your heart."

Evander thanked him, and looked out of the window, which gave a prospect of a small lawn not innocent
of croquet-rings and mallets, Alma being a devoted

admirer of the game, and her great grief a dearth of friends to play with her.

But Evander had strangely mistaken the character of Alma, who, when told by her father the object of the baronet's visit, begged him to return to his friend and inform him that she could never love him, and would not allow him to make any advances to her.

On hearing this Evander was furious; but neither threats nor entreaties could gain him an interview with the daughter of the old gentleman who bowed him out.

Going to the stable, he mounted his horse, tossed half-a-crown to the groom, and cantered away down the road which led to Brighton, with anything but a feeling of satisfaction.

CHAPTER XVII.

THE DESCENT OF THE AVALANCHE.

WE must leave the inmates of the farm to their own reflections, while we follow Sir Charles Evander to Brighton. His horse was flecked with foam when he drew up at the door of his hotel, his impatience of mind had made him press the poor creature to its utmost, and it was led panting away to the stables by an attendant.

" A gentleman to see you, sir. He has been waiting more than an hour. Here is his card," said a footman, as Evander entered the hotel.

He took the card, and reading the name of Dr. Rox said, " Very well; I will go to him," went to the apartments where the Doctor was awaiting his coming.

Dr. Rox did not rise when he entered; he was

L

smoking, and reading a magazine, which he threw aside, saying, "At last! You have been for a long ride."

"Yes," answered Evander laconically, as he took off his hat and gloves, and placed them in a corner.

"When does your mother's funeral take place?"

"The day after to-morrow. As you are so old a friend of the late Lady Evander, you will like to follow, I presume?"

"With your permission."

"O, you might be chief mourner, for all I care," answered Evander brutally.

"That is just the sort of speech I expected from you," said Dr. Rox calmly.

"And why from me?"

"Because it is impossible for you to feel that regard for Lady Evander which a son would have done."

"A son! What do you mean? Everybody knows I am her son," said Evander, becoming pale.

"Everybody thinks so; but I know you are not, and I can prove it."

"I am not in the humour for joking," said Sir Charles. "Postpone your pleasantries, if you please, for some more propitious time."

"It is not pleasantry," answered Dr. Rox; "I am stating the simple truth, and I came here on purpose to do so. Are you disposed to listen to me? It matters little, though, whether you are or not; for you must hear what I have to say sooner or later, and you may as well hear all now."

"Understand one thing, Doctor—"

"And that is—"

"I am not to be terrified into compliance with any wish of yours by the invention of a cock-and-a-bull story."

"O dear, no. I did not suppose you were, for an instant. I can support all I am going to say by evidence which in a court of law would be conclusive against you, and in favour of Mr. Noel Evander your cousin."

"Always that name?" said Evander in a tone of annoyance. "I had a presentiment when I first saw him, that he would be a thorn in my side."

"Your presumptive, or putative, father died suddenly, as you are aware," began Dr. Rox.

"Why repeat an old scandal? He died by his own hand, as I would die by mine if there was occasion for it," cried Evander testily.

"You will soon have an opportunity of using your discretion on that point," answered the Doctor, adding, "but to my story. When your presumptive father died, Lady Evander was in great dread lest the estates should pass from her to the next heir, because she was childless. She consulted me, and I suggested the procuration of a child. She fell in with my views. We circulated a report that she would soon be a mother, and she retired into the strictest privacy. I procured her a child, which was passed off as her own. You are that child; and you have usurped that property, which is legally Noel Evander's."

"If that is true," said Evander, whose pallor increased momentarily, "you were the accomplice in a rascally fraud."

"I was," answered the Doctor calmly; "and shall I tell you why?"

"If you will."

"I had a grave wrong to avenge upon Mr. Evander, the brother of the baronet, whose title and estates you inherit. He was brought up to the law, and occupied chambers in Doctors' Commons. He was my legal adviser, and he became acquainted with my wife. My kindness he requited in the most infamous manner. You shall hear why I vowed to have revenge upon him and his. Oblige me with a light, please. My cigar has gone out. Thank you. I know now that true wisdom consists in preventing a quarrel beforehand, rather than in avenging it afterwards; but the outraged feelings of a husband will not always admit of the application of wise saws.

"In years gone by," continued Doctor Rox, "I had passed the college and the hall, and had a good practice. I was happy and contented, with a moderate fortune at my disposal, and in every way my own master. I have reason to believe that all men, at some period of their lives, are susceptible of the charms of woman. I loved in a passionate and devoted manner. The object of my choice was well worthy of my adoration; a fairer or a better creature never existed. We were happy, until, in the way of business, I came in contact with Mr. Evander. That man, who, in spite of his smiling exterior, was an arch fiend—an offshoot of Satan—a diabolic fragment, which, in strict retribution, should have joined its parent carcass in the place where we are told there is weeping, wailing, and gnashing of teeth—that man was constantly at my house, on various pretexts; but I was not long in discovering that his visits were paid, not to me, but to my wife. She resisted his machinations and solicitations with all the firmness that should always belong to a good and virtuous woman. She repulsed him with scorn, and yet with dignity, on every occasion; but she was silly enough not to tell me of the

disgraceful advances and dishonourable proposals which
he had had the brazen audacity and the base ingratitude
to offer her. Had I known of his advances, I would
have strangled him as he sat in his chair at dinner; but
I was altogether ignorant of the man's perfidy. I was
cherishing a viper in my bosom, warming him by my
fireside, and nourishing him, until he found an opportunity of stinging me with all the violence of his poisonous
nature. I found it necessary, one day, to undertake a
journey which would necessitate an absence from home
of at least three days. My wife threw her arms round
my neck when the announcement was made to her, and
begged me to postpone it. The business upon which I
was going was important; so that I was unable to comply
with her request. Her tears began to flow afresh on
finding me obdurate. She assured me that she had a
presentiment of coming evil. I laughed at her fears,
and told her she would not be alone, because I had
invited Evander to come and see her as often as his
professional duties and engagements would allow him.
With a strange vehemence, which startled, while it
alarmed me, she declared that the society of any man
would be preferable to that of the one I proposed leaving
her in the charge of. I thought this objection was the
result of a silly prejudice—a whim, a caprice, one of
those fleeting fancies that women are so often the victims
of. If she had only possessed courage enough to have
gone a little further, and have initiated me into the cause
of her dislike, all would have been well, and a fearful
catastrophe averted; but this she did not do. As she
gave no reason for her dislike, I kissed her tenderly, as
was my custom, and took my departure, leaving her
upon the sofa in a half fainting condition, which I attri-

buted to her excessive affection for me, and her grief at
losing me even for a brief interval. I finished my business to my satisfaction, and returned home with open
arms, anticipating the most intense pleasure at once
more embracing the object of my affections. But what
was my horror and consternation at finding my house
shut up and deserted! Not a soul was to be seen. Mar-
velling much at so very unusual and extraordinary an
occurrence, I burst open the door. Nothing but vacancy
was revealed to my expectant gaze! My horror and
despair was something so exceptionally awful, that I
found myself at a loss for words wherewith to describe
it in a fitting manner. My wife was gone! Whither,
was a mystery to me as profound and black as night. I
threw myself on the ground, and gave way to a par-
oxysm of grief, such as is almost weak and cowardly in
a man, whose fortitude is supposed to be one of his chief
qualities. A season of black despair and gloom set in,
overshadowing my heart, and throwing a blight over my
hitherto happy and peaceful existence. I employed the
police to search for her, and I offered rewards, such as
would have tempted the cupidity of most people. But all
was unavailing ; I could hear no tidings of the lost one.
At length it occurred to me that the attorney of whom
my wife had spoken might have been instrumental in
her abduction. I hastened to him, questioned him,
threatened him; but without obtaining any satisfactory
reply to my eager queries. He either could not, or
would not speak. Of course, I afterwards knew the
cause of his silence. The scoundrel was afraid to admit
his villany! Had he confessed his guilt, I am positive
I should have tossed him out of the nearest window, and
have put an end to the existence of so worthless and

wicked a wretch. I may speak warmly; but I have been roused to vengeance by years of suffering and consciousness of injury. Evander had, since he first heard of my loss, been one of my most indefatigable consolers. He comforted me after the manner of those who ministered to Job in his afflictions; and preached a resignation which I had little inclination to indulge; indeed, if the truth must be told, my heart was hard, and stubborn, and rebellious. I was ready to go to war with every one. I was anxious to lift my hand in savage strife against one and all. Some one had wronged me grievously, foully, hideously; and I had a right to look for revenge. If I could not certify against some one particular individual, I would war against the whole human race. What use was it to exhort me to patience and submission? To every remark of that nature I responded in a firm voice,—' Give me back my wife, and I will be as docile as a lamb.' Three, four, five, six months passed—such weary, dreadful months! a time of great suffering, such as I trust very few have to pass through.

" One day, while leaving the business chambers of the attorney, an old woman accosted me, and from her I learned the startling particulars I was in search of. She, of course, gave me the information through hope of fee and reward. This was what she told me:— The attorney had abducted my wife during my absence in the country, and had confined her in some chambers near his own in Doctors' Commons. The unfortunate lady had resisted his overtures with courage beyond all praise; but at last her brain gave way, and she became hopelessly insane. Afraid to release her or send her away, lest I should gain a clue to her whereabouts, he kept her shut up in the same place. In

order to verify the truth of the woman's statement, I
summoned up all my resolution, and guided by her,
ascended the stairs which led to my wife's place of
captivity. I entered the room, and saw her sitting on
a chair. She turned her full and lustrous blue eyes
towards me; but there was not the slightest symptom
of recognition in the staring orbs. A glance was sufficient to convince me that my darling Zoe—my hope,
my idol, my adored Zoe—was nothing more or less than
the lawyer's mad prisoner. The shock stupefied me,
and I fell upon the floor insensible. When I came to
myself again, I found my wife standing by my side and
gazing curiously at me, as if I and my fainting-fit were
too much for her poor aberrated intellect to understand.
Raising myself up, I caught her by the hand and called
her by her name. The familiar accents of my voice
were strange and unknown to her now. She was totally
oblivious of my presence, and seemed to confound me
with the articles of furniture scattered about the apartment here and there. To her I was not at all superior
to a sofa, no better than a chair. It was a miserable
state for her to have fallen into. My plaintive appeal
to her memory was unsuccessful — the light of her
reason was extinguished for ever; and 'Zoe, Zoe,' had
no meaning for her bewildered intellect. With a cry
of intolerable anguish I threw myself once more upon
the ground, and writhed in unutterable anguish. I was
sick with love. My idol was before me; but she might
just as well have been fashioned out of wood or marble.
She was unconscious of my delicate feeling, and unable
to commiserate the terrible agony that I was under-
going. It was a sad and shocking day that, when I
saw my wife after our prolonged absence. I would

much rather I had never seen her again, but for one
reason; and that was—I knew who to regard as the
author of my misery. This filled me with exultation;
I had so much to revenge. Henceforth, I thought,
revenge shall be the whole business of my life! I
shouted, ecstatically—'Vengeance! vengeance!' until
the air rang with the sanguinary cry. I dwelt upon
the idea until the atmosphere was filled with daggers,
such as floated before Macbeth : and I longed to plunge
their poisoned tips into the heart of the attorney, and
keep them there up to the hilt. I could have ground
them round and round savagely, hearing the bone and
cartilage crack the while, and drinking up the sighs and
groans of my victim, as the gods above drink nectar.
Tearing myself away from the apartment which contained my unhappy wife, I rushed into the open air to
cool my heated brow and find surcease of sorrow. Vain
hope! delusive expectation! For me there was no
surcease of sorrow. My wife! without a mind : like a
beautiful statue. A piece of chiselled marble—a block
of well-cut stone—a tree, a shrub. a plant, a flower—
a thing of oils and canvas—would have made me such
a wife! My wife! As I repeated these two expressive
words to myself, my rage and frenzy broke out with
redoubled vigour, and I set myself to work to discover a means of punishing Evander for his unutterable
wickedness. At length my wife died, and was out of
her misery. And soon afterwards I had an opportunity
of plotting with Lady Evander to deprive my enemy
of the property which was legally his."

"Why, then, soften in favour of his offspring?"
asked Sir Charles.

"Because my heart is changed. I cannot war

against the innocent. Noel is a worthy young man, and has done me no harm; and it is my firm intention to make amends for the wrong I have done him. Lady Evander, on her death-bed, made a confession, which was taken down in writing by a competent and authorised person, in the presence of irreproachable witnesses. In it she states that you were substituted as her son. This confession is in my possession, and I intend to communicate its contents to Noel. If you like to give up your present position quietly, a certain income will be guaranteed you for life. If you fight us, you will inevitably be beaten in the end and get nothing."

Sir Charles Evander was like a ghost at the conclusion of this speech; his hands fell powerless by his side, and he made no reply.

Dr. Rox watched him narrowly.

"Come to me to-morrow," said Evander, after a pause; " I will think this matter over."

His manner was odd and strange, but Dr. Rox took his leave without another word, promising to call as requested.

During the remainder of the day, and the whole of the night, Evander sat up drinking brandy. He had no reason to disbelieve one word that Dr. Rox had told him; and seeing that his position, as well as his fortune, was gone, he, maddened by despair and drink, placed a pistol in his mouth and shot himself dead. Shocking as this event was, people only said that it was "in the family;" and as his father had done the same thing, he had merely acted upon a very natural impulse.

Dr. Rox's task was now simplified. To Noel's intense amazement and unbounded joy, he was informed that he was, by law and right, a baronet, and the possessor of a large fortune. Mr. Maitland withdrew his objection to him as a son-in-law; and by the timely interference of Dr. Rox the gloomy prospects of the Maitlands and the poor young man were changed as if by the waving of a magician's wand. The long-tangled skein was unravelled, and the fraud which had been perpetrated by Lady Evander and the mysterious Doctor was cleared up by that singular individual himself, who, without staying to enjoy the gratitude of the parties he had benefited, went abroad, and was never seen in England again. With him he took a blighted heart and a mind diseased, to which no man could minister.

Noel was very happy with his young wife, and the felicity they experienced in each other's society amply compensated them for all the misery of the past. Mr. Maitland forgave in wealth and rank what he had condemned in poverty; and he had now no fault to find in Sir Noel Evander, his lucky son-in-law.

At the death of the profligate Sir Charles, Lord Carisbrook was reconciled to his wife, and returned to England about the time that Mr. Mortimer was married to Miss St. Aubyn; on which occasion Captain Vavasour was his best man, and made himself immensely popular with the bridesmaids by presenting them with the handsomest lockets he could procure from Mr. Streeter's fashionable establishment. Whether Miss St. Aubyn felt Sir Charles's death or not is uncertain, but she rarely mentioned him, and her friends always avoided any allusion to his career.

Robson and Son, Printers, Pancras Road, N.W.